"Why are you torturing yourself?"

Nick asked himself. "Don't even think about it."

He tried not to. But he kept picturing Kristin, glowing and beautiful in a long white dress and veil, slowly walking up the aisle.

Waiting at the foot of the altar would be the man who would forevermore have the right to touch Kristin, to kiss her, to love her....

Nick gritted his teeth.

No. No. No!

Then what are you going to do about it?

What *could* he do? It was too late to do anything.

Was it?

Are you nuts? This is her wedding day. You had your chance. You blew it. And now it's too damned late to do a thing.

But she wasn't married yet. She wouldn't be married for eight more hours.

Opening the front door, he began to run.

He would never know until he tried.

Dear Reader,

April is the time for the little things...a time for nature to nurture new growth, a time for spring to begin to show its glory.

So, it's perfect timing to have a THAT'S MY BABY! title this month. *What To Do About Baby* by award-winning author Martha Hix is a tender, humorous tale about a heroine who discovers love in the most surprising ways. After her estranged mother's death, the last thing Caroline Grant expected to inherit was an eighteen-month-old sister...or to fall in love with the handsome stranger who delivered the surprise bundle!

And more springtime fun is in store for our readers as Sherryl Woods's wonderful series THE BRIDAL PATH continues with the delightful *Danielle's Daddy Factor*. Next up, Pamela Toth's BUCKLES & BRONCOS series brings you back to the world of the beloved Buchanan brothers when their long-lost sister, Kirby, is found—and is about to discover romance in *Buchanan's Return*.

What is spring without a wedding? *Stop the Wedding!* by Trisha Alexander is sure to win your heart! And don't miss Janis Reams Hudson's captivating story of reunited lovers in *The Mother of His Son*. And a surefire keeper is coming your way in *A Stranger to Love* by Patricia McLinn. This tender story promises to melt your heart!

I hope you enjoy each and every story this month!

Sincerely,

Tara Gavin,
Senior Editor

Please address questions and book requests to:
Silhouette Reader Service
U.S.: 3010 Walden Ave., P.O. Box 1325, Buffalo, NY 14269
Canadian: P.O. Box 609, Fort Erie, Ont. L2A 5X3

TRISHA ALEXANDER

STOP THE WEDDING!

Silhouette®

SPECIAL EDITION®

Published by Silhouette Books
America's Publisher of Contemporary Romance

For Chris Wenger: Thanks for your humor, your daily e-mail, your support and understanding, and most of all, your friendship. One of these days I expect to see your name on the cover and my name in the dedication.

 SILHOUETTE BOOKS

ISBN 0-373-24097-X

STOP THE WEDDING!

Copyright © 1997 by Patricia A. Kay

TRISHA ALEXANDER

has had a lifelong love affair with books and has always wanted to be a writer. She also loves cats, movies, the ocean, music, Broadway shows, cooking, traveling, being with her family and friends, Cajun food, Calvin and Hobbes, and getting mail. Trisha and her husband have three grown children, three adorable grandchildren and live in Houston, Texas. Trisha loves to hear from readers. You can write to her at P.O. Box 441603, Houston, TX 77244-1603.

The honor of your presence is
cordially requested

on Saturday, the tenth of June

at St. Paul's Episcopal Church

at the marriage of

Kristin Forrest Blair to...

...?*

*Groom to be announced forthwith

R.S.V.P.

Prologue

From the pages of the Green River Gazette

"Around the Town"
by Deena Bartholomew

Our town has been eagerly awaiting the much-heralded wedding of Kristin Forrest Blair and Douglas Jessup Llewellyn, which will take place two weeks from Saturday at St. Paul's Episcopal Church, with a reception following at the Green River Country Club. As you all know, Kristin is one of the beautiful Blair girls—the oldest daughter of Edmond and Meredith Blair, one of Green River's most prominent families and the owners of Blair Manufacturing.

Doug is the son of Bill and Cecily Winthrop Llewellyn, and holds the position of Vice President of Operations at Blair Manufacturing, where one of my "town spies" tells me he is the fair-haired boy and slated to take over as president when Edmond Blair retires.

Other spies tell me Kristin's wedding gown will knock our eyes out. What it looks like is a closely guarded secret, but I can tell you it was designed by Priscilla of Boston and does full justice to Kristin's delicate blond beauty. Sigh.

Nick Petrillo stared at the gossip column, which went on in this vein for several more fawning paragraphs. Emotions he'd thought long buried pushed up out of his past to engulf him.

Bitterness, pain and anger vied for domination. The anger won out as he swept the newspaper and its offending article off his desk in a gesture furious as well as futile, since there was no one in his office to witness it.

Clenching his jaw, he stalked over to the big window that overlooked Wall Street to the southwest and Nassau to the north. Normally, the busy streets below served as a soothing reassurance of his brilliant success in the financial capital of the world and reminded him of how far he'd come from his less-than-desirable origins.

But today, with just a few printed words, he'd been rudely thrust back to the days when he was nobody.

Less than nobody.

Trash.

"You're trash, boy, not fit to lick the shoes of my daughter, let alone marry her!" Edmond Blair had said, lip curling in distaste.

Nick closed his eyes.

He was no longer the kid from Green River, Connecticut, whose father was the town drunk and whose mother cleaned the toilets of rich people. He was no longer the upstart who thought he could actually have the daughter of the town's most prominent citizen.

He opened his eyes. Gazed down again. This time the view worked its magic. He was once more Nick Petrillo, boy wonder. Wall Street's whiz kid. The manager of the single most successful mutual fund to dazzle the financial world in recent years—a man who had the kind of genius to triple and quadruple fortunes.

At the age of thirty-two he earned a seven-figure income, owned a showplace three-bedroom apartment on East 66th St. near Madison Avenue, and numbered among his acquaintances most of the young movers and shakers in New York.

So what if Kristin Blair was getting married?

So what if he had once given her his heart and she had trampled on it?

So what if she had hurt him and betrayed him and lied to him?

Those days were long gone. Twelve years had passed since he'd last seen Kristin, and he was not the same person. He didn't have to take a back seat to anyone. He had accomplished great things. He had made it in one of the most competitive environments existing anywhere, among brilliant and accomplished people.

Yet even as he told himself all of this, he knew it wasn't enough.

It would never be enough.

Not until Kristin Blair and her arrogant bastard of a father were made to suffer as he'd been made to suffer would Nick be satisfied.

For years he had dreamed of the day he'd return to Green River, of the satisfaction he'd feel when he had destroyed Edmond Blair and his family the way they'd tried to destroy him.

Then, and only then, could he put the past where it belonged.

Nick strode back to his desk. Stared at the phone for a long moment. Then he picked up the receiver and punched the intercom for his secretary.

"Paula?" he said when she'd answered. "Cancel all my appointments for the next two weeks. I'm going out of town in the morning." He paused. Listened. "It's personal," he answered in a tone that did not invite further questioning.

When he hung up the phone, he smiled.

Chapter One

"Which one should I wear tonight?" Kristin Blair asked. She held up two cocktail dresses—a sequined red chiffon and a ruffled black taffeta.

"Definitely the red one," her younger sister Brooke said.

"I don't know." Kristin studied the red dress doubtfully. "Blondes aren't supposed to wear red."

Brooke laughed. "Why did you ask me if you didn't want my opinion?"

Kristin smiled. Brooke always made her smile. "You really think the red?"

"Yes, I do. You're right, *some* blondes can't wear red, but we're lucky. We don't have that washed-out look. So we can wear fire-engine red if we want to." She grinned, stretching out full-length on Kristin's canopied bed, but carefully, because she was almost

seven months pregnant and beginning to get un-
wieldy, although in every other way, she looked
wonderful. Her skin glowed and her blue eyes sparkled in the sunlight cascading through the bay windows fronting the Blair estate.

It would be easy to be jealous of Brooke, thought
Kristin, except that her younger sister was so nice
and so generous and so happy, you couldn't help
being happy for her.

"Why'd you buy the dress, anyway, if you thought
it wasn't a good color for you?" Brooke said.

Kristin grimaced. "You know me. I'm a soft
touch. And Mae Zelinsky talked me into it."

Brooke laughed. "I swear, if she wanted to, Mae
could sell the Brooklyn Bridge. But this time she was
right. Trust me. Wear the red. Red is a whole lot
sexier than black. Doug will want to jump your bones
when he sees you."

Kristin gave her sister an obligatory return smile.
She wasn't sure Doug Llewellyn would ever be eager
to "jump her bones," as Brooke had put it. For as
long as she'd known him, he had seemed to reserve
all of his stronger emotions and desires for his business deals.

For about the hundredth time, she wondered if she
were doing the right thing in marrying him. She
wasn't in love with Doug, and she didn't think he
was in love with her, even though he'd said the
words.

*At least I've never lied to him. I've never said I
loved him.*

Kristin no longer believed in love. What was the phrase so popular now?

Been there. Done that.

Yes. She had been there and done that, and look where it had gotten her.

Look *what* it had gotten her.

Heartbreak.

Agony.

Hurt beyond hurt.

True enough, but it also got you Lindsay.

The thought of Lindsay brought a powerful rush of love. Lindsay. To all the outside world, Lindsay Blair was Kristin's eleven-year-old sister, the last of the "beautiful Blair girls." Even Lindsay believed the fiction so hastily concocted by Kristin's parents.

Oh, my darling, did I do the right thing?

As always, when Kristin began doubting her choices, she shoved her misgivings away. What was done was done. Nothing could change the past, so there was no sense gnashing her teeth over her youthful folly or the path she'd chosen. The important person in this whole sordid story was Lindsay, and she was happy and secure. That was what counted.

"Why so pensive?" Brooke asked. "You having prewedding jitters?"

Kristin shrugged. "Something like that."

Brooke sat up carefully, ever mindful of her pregnant state. Her eyes were earnest as they met Kristin's. "Kris, listen, I've been thinking...."

"That's dangerous," Kristin teased. She walked to the closet that took up one whole wall of her bedroom and carefully hung up the dresses.

"No, listen, seriously…"

"All right, seriously…what have you been thinking about?" She fingered the satin folds of her wedding dress, which was hanging on the back of the opened closet door. She wished the sight of the beautiful dress brought her more pleasure.

"You know," Brooke said slowly, "marriage is so important. Believe me, living with someone else…well, it's very different from dating them. It's *hard.* Even the littlest things can irritate you, and if you don't truly *adore* someone… Well, what I'm trying to say is, if you're not sure you want to marry Doug, it's not too late to change your mind."

As her sister spoke, tears filled Kristin's eyes. She blinked rapidly, willing herself not to cry. Ever since accepting Douglas Llewellyn's proposal six months earlier, Kristin had toyed with the idea of backing out of the marriage more times than she could count.

Yet she always reached the same conclusion. She wanted more out of life than she had. She wanted children she could openly acknowledge as her own. And since she didn't expect—or even want—to fall in love again, Doug Llewellyn was a perfect choice for a husband.

He was steady, reliable and hardworking. He came from the same kind of family background and had the same kind of values. He had money of his own, so Kristin's money was not the reason for his interest in her, unlike someone else's had been, she thought bitterly.

Doug wanted children, too, and her parents approved of him wholeheartedly. And most importantly, Green River was his home and would remain his home.

Kristin could not leave Lindsay.

She could never leave Lindsay.

Lindsay was the reason Kristin, at twenty-nine, still lived in her parents' home. She was also the reason Kristin had gotten her teaching degree at a local university where she could commute on a daily basis instead of going away to college as she'd always imagined she would.

As long as Lindsay was in Green River, Kristin would be in Green River.

So she always came to the same conclusion. Doug would make her a good husband. They could build a good life. She was doing the right thing.

But even as she reminded herself of all this, a tiny secret part of her heart ached. If only she could claim Lindsay as her own. If only she could tell Doug the whole story. If only they could start their married life with total honesty and a clean slate.

"Kris?" Brooke murmured. "You okay?"

Kristin hastily nodded. "Yes," she managed to answer in a steady voice. Taking a deep breath, she turned and walked to the bed. She sat on one corner and reached for Brooke's hand. "Thanks for being so concerned."

Brooke nodded, but her eyes were thoughtful. "I just, you know, think you *deserve* to be happy, the way Chandler and I are happy. So if you have doubts…"

Kristin smiled and shook her head. "No. It's okay. I might have had some doubts earlier—I *did* have some earlier—but I don't any longer. So please don't worry about me. I'm going to be just fine. Just fine.''

Nick Petrillo drove slowly past the sign at the Green River city limits. During the three-hour trip from New York, he'd gone over his plan dozens of times, and in the process had gotten his emotions under steely control.

His plan was perfect.

He smiled with anticipation. Revenge had been a long time coming but would be all the sweeter for the wait.

First things first, though. He needed to find a place to stay. He wondered if Green River had become any more cosmopolitan during the past twelve years. When he'd left, there hadn't been a hotel or a motel in town. There'd been one boardinghouse on Elm Street and a bed-and-breakfast place on River Drive. Of the two, if the bed-and-breakfast still existed, he would consider staying there. If it didn't, he might have to backtrack and stay at the motel he'd noticed on the highway a few miles outside of town, even though it hadn't looked very appealing.

He drove slowly along Main Street, scanning the storefronts, noticing that most of the establishments looked a bit older and a bit seedier. The few new businesses were mostly fast-food restaurants.

Typical small eastern town, he thought. Hit hard by the changes wrought by so much foreign competition. He knew that the main employer in the area—one Blair Manufacturing—had downsized its workforce by more than forty percent in the past five years.

While I was going up, he *was going down.* And Edmond Blair would soon be going down even farther.

The sign for River Drive loomed ahead. Nick turned left, and as he did, a pedestrian stared at his car. He smiled. He'd be willing to bet the woman had never seen a Lamborghini before. *Take a good look, lady, I won't be around here long.*

River Drive ran parallel to the Green River, which looked surprisingly clean and unpolluted. It sparkled under the October sun, with the unusual green cast that had given it its name.

This was a pretty part of town, Nick allowed, especially at this time of year. The road was bordered with a profusion of maple trees whose leaves were at their peak of autumn finery—a riotous mixture of burgundy, scarlet, and orange and every shade in between.

Sometimes, living in the heart of Manhattan, surrounded as he was by concrete and steel, he forgot how pretty the countryside could be. Maybe one of these days he'd buy a weekend house in Westchester or the Hamptons.

He peered down the street. Good. There was the old familiar sign. Mary Ann's Bed & Breakfast. Underneath the larger, scrolled name, it said Serving The Best Homemade Biscuits In The State.

Nick's mouth watered, reminding him he hadn't eaten lunch. He wondered if D'Amato's Restaurant was still around. They used to have the best ravioli and pizza for miles.

Well, first he'd get a room, then he'd go on a food search.

He parked the Lamborghini in the driveway of the bed-and-breakfast. No way he was chancing getting it scratched or dented by leaving it on the street. Then he walked up onto the shallow porch of the old Victorian house and rang the bell, even though he could see the screened door was open.

From somewhere inside, a small dog barked and a woman said, "Shush, Poopsie. Now what did I tell you about barking?"

Moments later, the screened door was opened by a middle-aged woman with a friendly smile. "Yes? May I help you?"

"Hi," Nick said, returning her smile. "I'm looking for a place to stay for the next couple of weeks. Have you got a room available?"

"No, sorry," she said with obvious regret. "I'm full up right now."

"Damn," Nick muttered. "I don't suppose you know of anything else that might be available?"

"You say you need something for a couple of weeks?" The woman's thoughtful gaze moved past him to the Lamborghini. You could practically see the dollar signs in her eyes. "Tell you what. Why don't you go talk to Glenda at Albritton Realty? They're just up the street about two blocks. She might be able to help you."

Glenda Albritton, huh? Nick remembered her. He remembered her well. She'd been a hot number in high school. Had even given him the eye a couple of times, but he'd never been in a position to take her up on her interest. Hers or anyone else's. Dating a girl took money, and Nick had never had any.

"Thanks. I'll do that."

He smiled as he walked back to his car. Glenda Albritton. It would be interesting to see how she'd turned out.

A few minutes later Nick walked into the realty office. A pretty blond receptionist said, "Oh, you mean Mrs. Carroll," when he asked for Glenda. "I'll buzz her for you."

Moments later, a model-thin redhead with sultry golden brown eyes, dressed impeccably in a pale yellow wool suit, walked into the reception area. "Hello," she said, extending her right hand and giving him a practiced smile. "I'm Glenda Carroll. What can I do for you?"

Nick stood. Smiled. Took her hand and shook it firmly. "Hello, Glenda. I see you don't remember me."

Her eyes narrowed as she carefully looked him up and down. "You *do* look familiar, but I'm embarrassed to say I don't know why."

"Don't be. I've changed a lot since high school. Nick Petrillo."

Her eyes widened. Now her smile was brilliant. "Nick! Holy smoke. I *guess* you've changed." She gave a low whistle.

Nick grinned at her lack of inhibition. "Thanks...I guess."

"Let's go back to my office where we can talk. I

can't believe it. Nick Petrillo! You look like you hit the lottery...or something.''

"It's *or something*," he said dryly, following her lithe figure down a carpeted hallway and around to the right where she led him into a large corner office filled with sunlight and French antique furniture.

"Have a seat. Would you like some coffee? Or a drink? I've got some J & B and Stolichnaya.'' She headed toward a delicate rosewood sideboard whose surface held several crystal decanters and a silver coffee service.

"Coffee would be great.'' He sat in one of the two Louis XV armchairs placed in front of her desk and looked around with pleasure. The agency was obviously doing well if the caliber of furnishings and objets d'art were any indication. He particularly admired a small Lalique cat adorning her desktop and doubling as a paperweight.

Once she'd gotten them both cups of coffee and was settled behind the desk, she said, "What brings you back to Green River?''

"Business.''

"Oh?'' Her topaz eyes were frankly curious.

"I'll be here for about two weeks.'' He purposely did not elaborate on the nature of his business. "Mary Ann at the bed-and-breakfast suggested you might be able to help me find a place to stay.''

She leaned back in her chair, pursing her lips. "Two weeks. Hmm. That's tough. Most people want someone to stay longer.... I don't think...but wait a minute. Maybe I *can* help you. Would you be willing to pay a premium price?''

"Depends. How much are we talking about?"

"Well, a really beautiful small house in the City-side area is available—fully furnished. The rent is three thousand dollars a month. If you were willing to pay for a month and still allow me to show it to prospective tenants, I think the owner might agree to let you have it."

Cityside. That was where all of the old money in Green River lived. That was where Edmond Blair and his family lived.

"Done," Nick said.

"Tell you what. If you don't mind going back out to the reception area, I'll call the owner now. If she agrees, I'll take you over there immediately."

An hour later, the deal was clinched, and Nick found himself in possession of the keys to a beauti-fully renovated home that had apparently once been the carriage house for the larger estate next door. It was even furnished to his taste, with a blend of com-fortable, traditional furniture and interesting modern pieces.

"Thanks a lot," he told Glenda as he looked around the well-appointed living room. "It's per-fect."

"It is, isn't it?" She smiled, her eyes speculative. "So, Nick, what do you plan to do for fun while you're gracing our town with your presence?"

He shrugged. "I haven't thought about it."

"Well, I've got a suggestion. I'm on the commit-tee for the annual symphony benefit, and tonight's the big dinner-dance. I was supposed to go with Keith Ferguson—remember him?—but his grandmother died suddenly yesterday morning, and he left earlier today to fly to Orlando for the funeral, so I'm currently without an escort. Why don't you come with me?''

"I take it Mr. Carroll is out of the picture?''

She rolled her eyes. "Thank God. I've been divorced for three years.''

Nick didn't have to think about her offer very long. A benefit dinner for the Green River Symphony meant attendance by every mover and shaker in town, including the Blairs. "In that case, I accept. Only, I didn't bring a tux with me.''

"Doesn't matter. Lots of men will be wearing suits.'' She flashed him another of her big smiles. "Pick me up at seven.'' She gave him her address, which was in an area he recognized. When she walked away, he could hear her murmuring, "Nick Petrillo. My, my, my…''

After Brooke left to go home, Kristin curled up on the cushioned window seat of the big bay window in her bedroom and tried to shake her melancholy. A naturally optimistic person, she told herself to count her blessings and focus on the positive things in her life. For some reason, today those old standbys didn't work.

Sighing deeply, she gazed out at the autumn landscape. The Blair mansion sat on three acres of impeccably manicured lawn dotted with stately maple, elm, pine and birch trees. Today, two men from the lawn-care service her parents used were raking leaves, and another was mulching flower beds in preparation for the winter.

Exactly two weeks from today she would become Mrs. Douglas Jessup Llewellyn, and she would leave her parents' home forever. She thought about the house waiting for her—the house she and Doug had chosen together. He had moved into it six weeks ago, when the builders had finished the last of the interior work. If only the prospect of joining him there brought her the same kind of excitement and joyous anticipation she had once felt about sharing a home with someone else.

Stop it! she told herself. Stop thinking about the past. Stop tormenting yourself. The past is over and done with. And you should be glad, not sad. You wouldn't have wanted to spend your life with someone who cared more for money than he did for you, so things worked out for the best. But no matter how many times she lectured herself, the words failed to bring her comfort.

The problem was, her upcoming wedding had brought back memories she'd thought long since dealt with and banished. Well, never *completely* banished, because Lindsay was a constant reminder of the past. But Kristin had truly believed the pain of Nick Petrillo's desertion was gone. And now, these past few months had proven to her that it wasn't.

Restless and unhappy, she jumped up, walked over to the closet and took out a jacket. Then she grabbed her purse and hurried out.

She took the back stairs. She didn't think her mother was home, but she was taking no chances. If her mother saw her, she would be sure to ask where Kristin was going and she did not want to be questioned.

She was in luck. The only person she saw was Milly, the family's live-in housekeeper. Milly looked up from folding towels and smiled as Kristin passed.

"Bye, Milly." Kristin waved. "I'm going out for a while. See you later."

"Bye, Miss Kristin."

She pointed her little green Mazda toward Primrose Hill, the place that had been her refuge from the moment she was old enough to drive. At its crest stood an enormous copper beech tree, and when Kristin sat under its sheltering branches, she could see all of the Green River valley spread out before her like the colorful pieces of a quilt.

The spire of the Congregational Church and the top of the First National Bank were easily identifiable, as were the sprawling buildings that housed Blair Manufacturing, the high school, the football stadium, the golf course and the adjoining country club.

Primrose Hill was the place where Kristin had worked out her knottiest problems. It was also the place where she and Nick Petrillo, the first and only man she'd ever loved, had always met. It was there they'd first made love, and it was there he'd asked her to marry him.

And it was there she'd sobbed her heart out after he'd left her.

Twenty minutes later, Kristin rounded the last curve before the summit. She pulled off the road and walked toward the huge old tree that dominated the landscape. Its smooth, gray bark still bore the remnants of the initials carved there so long ago: *NP & KB*.

Kristin's sad eyes gazed at the physical reminder of the man she'd once trusted so completely, she'd given him everything: heart, body, soul.

She sank down, her back against the tree trunk. Then she closed her eyes and let the memories come.

The first time she'd seen Nick was the August before her senior year of high school. She had just turned seventeen in June, and she was impossibly romantic. Her two favorite pastimes were reading the novels of Jane Austen and the Brontë sisters and watching old movies on television. She always imagined herself in the role of the heroine.

Someday, she told herself, someday I'll meet the man of my dreams, too.

That night, a sultry Friday in late August, she and Susan Rosenbaum, a classmate and part of Kristin's crowd, went downtown to the movies. Susan was the first one to notice the dark-haired, dark-eyed, handsome boy behind the refreshment counter.

"That's Nick Petrillo," she said in a stage whisper. "Isn't he the *coolest?* He was in Edward's class." Edward was Susan's older brother.

"Hi, Nick," Susan said as they walked up to the counter.

"Hello, Susan."

"How are you?"

"I'm fine," he said. "How are you?"

"Fine. Um, I'll have some Gummi Bears and a Coke."

"Okay." He looked at Kristin.

Kristin's heart gave a little hop as she gazed into Nick Petrillo's dark eyes. "I—I'll have a bag of popcorn and a Coke," she said.

"Buttered?" He didn't smile.

She nodded, mesmerized by his eyes. They looked like a poet's eyes, she thought. Soulful. When he handed her the drink and the popcorn, their fingers brushed, and a little jolt of electricity zapped her. He felt it, too, because his eyes met hers again, and this time, he did smile. A slow, intimate smile that did things to her stomach.

"What's *your* name?" he said.

"Oh, sorry," Susan said. "This is Kristin Blair. Kristin, this is Nick Petrillo."

"Hello, Kristin Blair."

Kristin swallowed. His voice was like velvet. Soft, low, sexy. "H-hi." Oh, she could have kicked herself! What was *wrong* with her? Why couldn't she say something smooth and smart?

"That'll be two dollars and seventy-five cents," he said, still smiling at her.

She put down the drink and popcorn and counted out the money. She wished she was older and had more experience, because she knew, without a doubt, that she wanted to see Nick Petrillo again—somewhere other than here—but she had no idea how to go about engineering another meeting. "It was nice to meet you" was all she managed.

"Gawd, he's gorgeous, isn't he?" Susan said as

the two friends walked slowly into the darkened theater. "I always wanted to go out with him, but Edward said Nick didn't date much. 'Course, he was never interested in *me*, anyway." She gave Kristin a sidelong glance. "He seemed interested in *you*, though."

"Do you really think so?"

"Yeah, I do, but don't get your hopes up. According to Edward, Nick is saving every penny for college."

"Is he in college now?" Her heart sank. If he was in college, he would be leaving town any day now to go back to school.

"I don't know. Since Edward moved out, I don't see much of his friends."

All through the movie, Kristin thought about Nick Petrillo. Aside from the fact that if he were in college, he would be leaving Green River soon, why would he be interested in her, a girl who was just entering her senior year of high school? He probably had tons more sophisticated girls interested in him. It had probably been Kristin's imagination, that jolt of electricity and the accompanying jolt of awareness between them. He had probably already forgotten all about her.

But Nick hadn't forgotten all about her.

In fact, when she and Susan exited the theater, he was standing there, leaning against the wall near the exit doors. When he saw them approaching, he slowly walked toward them. He looked at Kristin. "You walking home or riding?"

Kristin could hardly answer, she was so flustered. "I, um, rode with Susan."

Now he looked at Susan. "Do you care if she goes with me?"

Susan looked at Kristin. *Do you want to?* her eyes said. Seeing Kristin's answer, she said, "No, I don't care."

Again he turned to Kristin. "Can I take you home?"

"All right," she said.

And that was the beginning.

Kristin sighed and slowly opened her eyes. She had fallen in love so quickly and so deeply. She would have done anything, given up anything, for him. Followed him anywhere. He was the center of her universe.

Even now, the pain of his betrayal cut so deep. She had believed in him totally. She had been so young. So naive. And so stupid.

Chapter Two

After unpacking his bags and hanging up his clothes, Nick headed out to his car. He was starving, and he hoped D'Amato's Restaurant was still around.

He was in luck. The popular eatery still stood on the corner of Elm and Third Streets.

Not much had changed in the past twelve years. He sniffed appreciatively as he entered the sunshine-filled dining room redolent with garlic, basil and several other mouth-watering aromas.

There were the same scarred wooden tables, the same red-checked tablecloths, the same half-burned candles in Chianti bottles and the same pictures of Italy on the walls.

Now, if only the food had remained as good as he remembered it, he would be a happy man.

Because it was past the normal lunch hour, there

were only a few occupied tables in the restaurant. Nick stood by the front counter, which contained the cash register, menus, and holders containing toothpicks and mints. A few minutes later, a plumpish woman with curly dark hair and a welcoming smile hurried toward him.

"Sorry to keep you waiting." She took a menu from the countertop. "Table for one?"

He smiled and nodded and followed her into the dining room.

She stopped by a table overlooking Elm Street. "This okay?"

"Great."

After handing him the menu, she studied him for a moment. "Don't believe I've seen you here before. You new in town?"

"No, not new, but I haven't been here in a long time. I ate here some when I was a kid."

"Really? I don't remember you." Her eyes narrowed thoughtfully. "Wait a minute. Are you...? No. You couldn't be."

Nick grinned as it dawned on him who the woman was. The twenty or so extra pounds she was carrying had thrown him off for a few minutes, but the smile and the lively blue eyes couldn't belong to anyone else.

He stuck out his hand. "Nick Petrillo. And you're Rosalie."

A flood of memories engulfed him. Rosalie D'Amato had dated his older brother Billy for a couple of years, and Nick had always liked her.

"Nick!" she exclaimed, shaking his hand. "I—I can't believe it! You look...*wonderful.*"

He grinned. "You look great, too."

She rolled her eyes in a self-deprecating gesture. "Yeah, sure. Maybe once I lose the weight I gained with my last baby, I'll look great, but for now..." Her voice trailed off. She shook her head and grinned at him. "Nick Petrillo. I still can't believe it. Where have you *been* all these years?"

"In New York."

"Really? New York." Her gaze took in his Italian loafers, designer jeans, fine wool sweater, eighteen-karat gold watch, and expensively cut and styled dark hair. "You've obviously done well."

"I can't complain."

"What do you do?"

"I work on Wall Street. Managing a mutual fund."

"Wow. That's great. I always knew you'd amount to something."

He'd always known he'd amount to something, too, despite the lack of faith certain people had shown. Well, he was the one who would soon be doing the showing, he thought with grim satisfaction.

"Gee," she said, continuing to study him with admiration. "It's so nice to see you again. You left Green River so suddenly. I figured you'd blown the town forever."

He gave her a noncommittal smile. "Tell me what you've been doing." Not only was he interested, but he preferred to change the focus of the conversation from himself to her. "I take it you're married."

Her eyes lit up. "Uh-huh. It'll be ten years next month, as a matter of fact. I married Ted Wachinska—do you remember him? He used to be the star pitcher for the Green River Bullfrogs?"

Nick recalled a tall, sandy-haired quiet boy with a great arm. "Sure do."

"We have three kids. Two girls, eight and six, and a little boy." Her voice softened. "Teddy will be six months old tomorrow."

The expression in her eyes caused Nick to feel a fleeting sense of loss, but he shook it off as she continued talking, telling him about her mother, who'd died two years earlier, and her father, who'd had a fatal heart attack six months later.

"It was hard to lose them both," she said sadly, "especially so close together, but..." She sighed. "Life goes on. My brother Dom and I are now running the restaurant. You remember him? He married Corinne Rooney. They've got two girls. One of the girls, Erin, she works here on the weekends. In fact, she'll be here at four. She's a sweetheart. I can hardly believe she's already sixteen. Gee, time flies, doesn't it?" Not waiting for his answer, she plunged on. "But listen to me going on and on about my family. What about yours? I know your father died. I, uh...I was sorry to hear about it." Her gaze skittered away. She had obviously remembered the circumstances surrounding his father's untimely ending.

Nick tried never to think about his father, because reminders only made him angry. Jim Petrillo's death was directly related to his weakness for the bottle, and everyone in town had known it.

The accident had happened two years after Nick left Green River, in a period of time when his father was working regularly. As was Nick's father's custom, he'd headed straight for his favorite beer garden after picking up his weekly paycheck, where he then proceeded to drink most of it away.

On this particular Friday it had been raining since noon, and by ten o'clock when Jim finally staggered out of the bar, the rain had turned to freezing sleet. He was walking home because Nick's mother had learned long before to be gone on payday, thereby depriving him of the use of the only car the family owned.

So, that night, on foot, he lurched his drunken way down the street. Later, when the hysterical call came from the woman who had hit him, the family was informed that Jim had simply fallen into the path of her car. There was nothing she could do, because by the time she saw him, it was too late.

Nick doubted anyone except his mother had shed a tear. Nick knew he certainly hadn't. And he had not returned to Green River for the funeral, although he would have, for his mother's sake, but she hadn't wanted him to. Nick had been secretly glad. He'd had no sympathy for his father. Not for his whining. Not for his contention that he was always unfairly treated. Not for anything. His father had been a weak, mean man who had blamed everyone else for his own shortcomings and who had made punching bags out of his wife and sons.

"What about your mother?" Rosalie said, finally breaking the awkward silence. "I know she moved away, 'cause I heard people talking about how much they hated losing her. How's she doing?'' She smiled. ''I always liked your mother.''

Nick smiled, too. Everyone had liked his mother. And no wonder. Peggy Petrillo was the kindest person he'd ever known as well as one of the hardest-working. It was one of the greatest satisfactions of Nick's life that his success had enabled him to give his mother an easier life.

''My mother is doing great. She lives in Albany now, with my sister Evelyn, and her family.''

''Oh, that's nice for her. And, um…Billy? Is he, um…?'' She seemed uncertain how to continue.

''Billy's straightened himself out. He's the assistant manager of an auto parts store. He's married, has a little boy and lives in Albany, too.''

Her smile was genuine. ''Oh, that's great. I'm really glad for him.''

Nick nodded. ''Me, too.'' For a while there, he wasn't sure his brother *could* straighten out his life, especially after his conviction for burglary, but eighteen months in jail, combined with a new maturity and Nick's financial help, had worked miracles. Billy had been straight for four years now.

''Do you see much of your family?''

''As much as I can.''

''You know,'' she said, ''the older I get, the more I realize how important family is.'' She made a face. ''Unlike when I was a kid, when I didn't even want to be seen in the same *room* with them.''

Nick smiled. ''We all grow up.''

''Yeah, thank goodness. Well, it's been great talking to you, Nick, but you wouldn't have come in here if you weren't hungry, so I guess I should let you look at the menu, huh?''

"I don't need to. I know exactly what I want. Spinach ravioli.''

"Good choice." She smiled at him again, took his menu and left.

While he waited for his food, he stared out the window. Seeing Rosalie, talking about their respective families, had underscored how different his life was now from what it had been when he'd lived in Green River.

He smiled ruefully, thinking about her comment that he'd left Green River so suddenly. Hell, anyone would have left town suddenly if they'd been threatened the way he'd been threatened.

He'd never forget that morning: the hard-eyed glare of Glen McCutcheon, the police chief, and the menace in McCutcheon's voice when he'd said, "Listen to me, Petrillo, and listen good. Get outta town *now*, because if you don't, I just might lock you up for good and throw away the key. And if you don't think I can do it, you just try me.''

Nick would never forget how helpless he'd felt.

He hadn't said a word.

Blindly, he'd stumbled out of the Green River Police Station into the hazy pink dawn of the June morning. He'd walked the six miles to the dilapidated frame house at the edge of town where he lived with his parents and younger sister.

When he got there, his father was snoring away in his usual drunken stupor, and his mother was tiptoeing around, trying to keep quiet while she got ready for work. Nick told her what had happened and what he planned to do, then he packed his clothes and his few belongings, kissed his mother and sister good-bye, and after promising to call when he was settled, left without a backward glance. He'd bummed a ride to the bus station with a neighbor.

As the bus ate up the miles between Green River and New York City, Nick had stared out the window while his mind went over and over everything that had happened to him.

In the space of days, he'd gone from a man who was planning to marry the most wonderful girl in the entire world to a man who'd been arrested on a trumped-up charge of suspicious behavior, thrown in jail, and then given a note she'd written saying she no longer wanted him.

Even today, so many years later, he could remember how his heart had hammered in denial as he read each cold, dream-destroying word.

This has all been a big mistake. I could never marry someone like you. Please don't try to see me again. I'm going to Europe with my parents. Kristin.

Her betrayal devastated him.

At first, he didn't believe it. He simply stared at the note and tried to breathe against the searing pain in his chest.

"Go on, call her up," Chief McCutcheon had said, as if he knew exactly what Nick was thinking and feeling. The sheriff had inclined his head toward the wall phone. "See for yourself. She's gone."

Nick wanted to smash his fist into McCutcheon's

smug, self-satisfied face. But some semblance of sanity remained in the fog of anger and hurt and disbelief. So instead of hurling himself at the sheriff, he pretended a calm he didn't feel and walked to the phone. There, with fingers he fought to keep from trembling, he dialed the familiar numbers. On the fourth ring, the Blair housekeeper answered. In a voice that didn't sound like his own, Nick asked for Kristin.

"Miss Kristin isn't here. None of them are here. The family has gone to Europe for the summer."

From that moment on, a new Nick Petrillo was born, the last remnants of his innocence destroyed. Over the years, Nick became polished, successful and powerful. A man who feared no one. A man who was always in perfect control. A man who had many acquaintances and no real friends.

But most importantly, a man who had never again allowed himself to be vulnerable to another human being…and who never would.

"Here we are," Rosalie said, breaking into Nick's thoughts. She laid a steaming platter of ravioli on the table in front of him. "Enjoy."

As Nick ate, he tried to empty his mind of the past. But no matter how hard he tried, he couldn't seem to stop the memories from coming.

By the time he'd finished his meal and said his goodbye to Rosalie, he knew he wasn't going to be able to banish them.

Not until he'd dealt with them.

All of them.

So he might as well get it over with.

Twenty minutes later, his powerful car roared up and around the last curve before the crest of Primrose Hill. He cursed softly as he saw the little green Mazda parked at the side of the road. Damn! Someone else was up here today, and he was in no mood for company. He debated turning around. He didn't have to do this today. He could come some other time when no one else was there.

"What the hell, I'm here," he muttered. "I'll just ignore whoever's up here." He pulled in behind the Mazda and cut the ignition.

Climbing out of the Lamborghini, he looked around. It was several degrees cooler up here, and the breeze carried the scent of the primroses that had given the hill its name. They were in full autumnal bloom, their white and yellow heads blowing gently in the wind. He couldn't help remembering how many times he'd picked a bunch of the flowers for Kristin and how she'd bury her face in them, as thrilled with his offering as if they'd been the most expensive hothouse roses. Often, over the years, he'd wondered if her reaction had been a lie, too, just as her profession of love and her promise to marry him had been lies.

He walked toward the south face of the hill, his gaze moving in the direction of the big beech tree where he'd once carved his and Kristin's initials.

He stopped abruptly.

Someone was there. A woman, sitting with her back against the tree.

Hell! Maybe he *would* leave and come back some

other time. As he wrestled with his decision, she got to her feet and slowly turned around.

The breath left Nick's body.

He felt as if someone had punched him in the gut. There, not ten feet away, looking just as stunned as he felt, stood the woman who had haunted his dreams for twelve years.

Kristin blinked twice.

Nick? No! It can't be. Oh, dear God.... It is. It's Nick.

She leaned against the tree for support, because her legs wanted to buckle under her.

Her mind whirled.

Nick Petrillo.

Here in Green River.

How could this be? Her mind didn't want to believe it. But there was no mistaking him. He had the same intense dark eyes, the same determined chin, the same thick, nearly black hair, and the same sensuous mouth, which had once had the power to reduce her to jelly.

She stared at him, unable to speak.

He, too, stood as if frozen.

Long moments passed.

Finally he spoke. "Hello, Kristin." There was no warmth in his voice or his eyes.

She swallowed. "H-hello, Nick." How handsome he looked. How mature and confident and polished. All the rough edges were gone. There was a casual arrogance about him that only the most successful and powerful men possess. Kristin should know.

She'd been around her father and his friends long enough, and they all had that look. "Y-you're looking well." *Why are you stammering, you idiot? Do you* want *him to know how rattled you are?*

She wanted to kick herself, but it was such a shock to see him, especially today, when he'd been so much in her thoughts.

In her wildest dreams, she had never expected to see Nick again. After what he'd done, she'd imagined he would be too embarrassed to ever return to Green River. Certainly too embarrassed to ever face her.

But here he was, and he didn't seem embarrassed or awkward at all. Only cold and formal and polite. As if he were talking to a stranger and not the woman he'd promised to love forever and then abandoned.

"You're looking well, too." His eyes studied her intently.

She couldn't seem to look away. Her heart tripped inside her chest like a frightened bird as unwanted emotions assailed her.

They'd spent so many nights up here on their hill, sitting by the tree, looking out over the town and talking about their dreams for the future.

How many times had they made love here? Twenty? Thirty?

She could still feel the roughness of the old blanket he'd kept in the trunk of his beat-up car, the one they laid on the ground when the weather was warm. She also remembered the warmth of the sleeping bag they cuddled into during the cold months. But most of all, she remembered what it was like when he touched her.

The memory of his hands on her body, his mouth against hers, was so real, she could almost feel them as if he were touching her now. And with the memory, the same desire flooded her—a heated rush that panicked her.

Oh, God, she prayed, *please help me, please, please, please help me....*

The knowledge that he still had the power to hurt her was devastating, for if he could still hurt her, she must still care.

All she wanted now was to escape, but she knew she couldn't just bolt and run, no matter how she felt. She would never give him the satisfaction of knowing how his unexpected reappearance had affected her.

Never.

She took a deep breath and, calling on all her strength, she forced a smile to her face. "This is certainly a surprise. I never expected to see you back in Green River. What are you doing here?"

He smiled cynically. "I'm sure you didn't."

His smile and tone of voice bewildered her. Why was he looking at her as if he hated her? She had done nothing to him. If anyone should be hating anyone, it should be her, because he was the one who had betrayed *her*, not the other way around.

"Why *are* you back?" she said.

The smile disappeared. "Why do you ask?"

She wanted to say something cold and cutting. But Kristin was a lady, raised to be polite under all circumstances. So she fixed a bright smile on her face and said, "No reason. I was just being polite." She slightly emphasized the word *I*.

"Meaning what? That I'm not?"

His attitude was beginning to make her mad. She had no idea why he was so angry, but she didn't intend to stand there and let him jab at her all day.

She shrugged, giving him the cool, slightly superior look she'd seen her mother level at rude people. "Take it any way you want to take it."

"I'm in town on business," he said curtly.

The thought crossed her mind that he might have returned to try to squeeze more money out of her father. But that was ridiculous. Her father would have no reason to give Nick more money.

She tightened her grip on her shoulder bag. "Well, I hope you enjoy your stay. It's been nice seeing you again, but I was just leaving." She couldn't resist adding, "I've got a million things to do to get ready for my wedding. I'm getting married in two weeks."

"To someone your daddy approves of, no doubt."

"Doug is a very nice person, yes," Kristin said stiffly, remembering how violently her father had disapproved of Nick. She knew he was remembering, too. She could see it in his eyes.

That hateful smile appeared again. "Your kind of people." His words were laced with contempt.

"If by 'your kind of people,'" Kristin said, stung by his scorn and finally goaded into retaliating, "you mean polite, thoughtful, generous and *honest*, well, yes, I guess you could say he's our kind of people."

Anger bubbled inside, and she welcomed it. She

would much rather feel anger than pain any day of the week.

"Look who's talking about honesty." His eyes, which had, in the past, always looked at her so warmly, were like the winter sky at night—icy and dark and forbidding. "A woman who doesn't know the meaning of the word."

Kristin knew she should just leave. This conversation, if you could call it that, was quickly deteriorating. But she couldn't let his insult go unchallenged. "Unlike you, I don't say things I don't mean, so where you get off saying that I'm dishonest, I can't imagine. And frankly, I don't care."

Heart pounding, she brushed past him, walking away as quickly as she could without actually running.

When she reached her car, her fingers shook as she searched for her keys. Finally she managed to find them in the front compartment of her purse and get her car unlocked. Practically sobbing with relief, she climbed in, started the car and made the U-turn necessary to drive away.

She knew he was standing there watching her.

She didn't look back.

Chapter Three

Nick watched her walk away and battled the demons raging inside.

It was incredible how, in the space of minutes, she'd stripped away the protective barrier he'd worn for years and uncovered all his raw emotions.

Her insinuation that *he* was dishonest when she'd been touting the virtues of her fiancé had infuriated him. Where did she get off saying something like that when *she* was the one who'd run out, leaving *him* to rot in jail?

Distractedly, he ran his fingers through his hair. Damn her! Even after all these years, she still had the power to make him crazy. He knew he would never forget the way she'd looked standing there today: blond hair shimmering in the sunlight, eyes as blue as the October sky, slender body tantalizing in tailored charcoal wool pants and matching sweater, a dark red blazer slung carelessly over her shoulders.

For a long time he had been telling himself his memories of Kristin were greatly romanticized. He'd imagined—no, he'd secretly *hoped*—the years had changed her for the worse.

Today had shown him how wrong he'd been.

The years had changed her, all right, but they'd changed her for the better. She was more beautiful now than she'd ever been.

The Kristin he'd loved twelve years ago had been a girl—a lovely, passionate girl. The Kristin he'd confronted today was a stunningly beautiful woman.

And he'd wanted her.

The knowledge shamed him.

How he could want her, after what she'd done to him, was a huge joke played on him by a laughing entity. But he had. Even so, he would sooner have cut off his arm than let her know it. He would *never* let her know it. He would cast her from his thoughts and master this weakness in himself if it was the last thing he ever did.

"I *will* conquer this," he muttered again and again as he walked to his car, then drove back to town. By the time he reached the rental house, he was calmer. He'd managed to convince himself he was making too much of what had happened today.

So he'd wanted her.

So what?

He'd wanted *dozens* of women over the years. Big deal.

The thing to do now was forget about today and concentrate on his reason for being in Green River.

He smiled grimly.

The next stockholders' meeting of Blair Manufacturing would take place the day before Kristin's wedding, and he would be there. He could hardly wait. He'd planned this moment for years. He had imagined the shock on Edmond Blair's face a thousand times, the fear that would follow when Edmond realized Nick was the new majority stockholder, and that he intended to wrest control of the company away from Edmond.

Yes, Nick thought with satisfaction, yes.

Let Edmond Blair be afraid as Nick had once been afraid. Let Edmond Blair feel the impotence and pain and desperation he and his cronies had mercilessly visited upon a kid who had never done anything more than fall in love with one of their daughters. Let Edmond Blair suffer as Nick had suffered.

Oh, yes.

Nick was going to enjoy this. He would enjoy it very much. It had been a long time coming, but he would soon have his revenge.

He would bring Edmond Blair and his daughter to their knees, and he would laugh in their faces before he walked away.

Kristin fought tears all the way home. She knew she had to get herself under control before she reached the house, because she could not let her family see her this way. If anyone were to see how upset she was, there would be questions.

Questions she didn't want to answer.

But it was so hard to calm down when your mind was whirling like a top. When you were still in a state of disbelief and shock. When you could hardly grasp the fact that the man you'd thought was safely out of your life forever had suddenly appeared again, rocking your world and shattering your hard-won serenity.

It was still almost impossible to grasp.

Nick Petrillo back in Green River.

What was he *doing* there? She knew his family no longer lived in the area. Enough of her parents' friends had employed Nick's mother for Kristin to have heard when Peg moved away, and of course, everyone had known about his father's accident. Something like that didn't happen in a town as small as Green River without it being common knowledge.

So why was Nick there?

He couldn't have come for a class reunion or anything like that. His class had had their reunion in the summer. Kristin had read the notice in the newspaper.

He'd said business. What kind of business? She knew his family had never owned any property in Green River, so his return could have nothing to do with settling an estate, or anything.

As she discarded possibilities, the most awful thought struck her. Could Nick be *moving* back to Green River? Maybe investing in a business here? Her heart skittered in panic.

Oh, dear God, surely not....

But what if he *was* moving back? What would she

do? The thought of constantly bumping into him, of always having to be on guard in case she did, and of the horrible possibility that somehow, someway, he might guess about Lindsay, was terrifying.

Calm down, calm down. At this rate, you'll never be able to go home.

She drove aimlessly up and down streets, talking to herself and fighting frightened tears. Finally, forty-five minutes after leaving Primrose Hill, she felt composed enough to face her family.

Even so, she prayed her mother would not yet be home from her bridge group. She just couldn't face her mother right now. Meredith was too astute, too in tune with her daughters and their emotions. She would know something was wrong and she would be relentless in ferreting out what it was.

Kristin's prayer was answered. Meredith's bronze Mercedes was gone from its slot in the three-car garage as Kristin pulled into the neighboring slot. "Thank you, God," Kristin whispered.

Before getting out of the car, she powdered her nose and applied fresh lipstick. The face staring back at her from the mirror looked acceptably normal.

Kristin walked to the house and let herself in the back door. She could hear Milly humming in the kitchen. "Hi, Milly," she called. "I'm back."

She headed for the back stairs without stopping. Even though she felt she could have survived Milly's scrutiny, she just wanted to escape to the safety and privacy of her room.

Unfortunately, she wouldn't be able to hide out very long. She and Doug, as well as her parents and

Brooke and Brooke's husband, Chandler, were all going to the Green River Symphony Benefit tonight.

Kristin wished she didn't have to go, but there was no way she could beg off. She was on the planning committee and would be seated at the head table. She would practically have to be on her deathbed before she could skip tonight's festivities.

There was no hope for it. She would have to go, and somehow she would have to get through the evening without arousing anyone's suspicion that there was anything amiss.

The first thing she saw when she entered her bedroom was the red cocktail dress she planned to wear that evening. Kristin stared at the dress, remembering her conversation with Brooke earlier today. That conversation could have taken place in another world, she thought wearily. Her biggest worry then was the uncertainty about her feelings for Doug. Now, scant hours later, that concern seemed miniscule after the discovery that Nick Petrillo was back in town.

The fear she'd successfully battled back threatened to take over again. Tossing her purse on the bed, she walked to the window and stared out sightlessly.

If only she knew what had brought Nick to Green River.

If only she were sure that his return had nothing to do with her...or her family.

She swallowed, the fear she'd temporarily tamped down rising up to engulf her again. Her chest felt tight and her heart was beating too fast.

Until she knew, without a doubt, that he posed no threat to her or Lindsay's well-being and security,

Kristin knew she would not draw another easy breath.

"Oh, good, you're home," said a voice behind her. "I was hoping you were."

Kristin took a second to steel herself before turning to smile at the person who meant more to her than anyone else in the world. "Hi, sweetie."

Lindsay, a beautiful youngster who looked uncannily like Kristin had looked at the same age except for her dark eyes, smiled back. But the smile slowly faded into a look of concern. She walked closer, frowning. "What's wrong, Krissie?"

Tenderness flooded Kristin. They had always been sensitive to the other's emotions. She should have known she couldn't hide her distress from Lindsay. "Nothing important," she lied. "Nothing to worry about."

"Are you sure?"

Kristin nodded. "I'm sure."

Seeing Lindsay after just having seen the man who was responsible for her existence was nearly Kristin's undoing. From the moment she'd held the tiny newborn in her arms, she had loved her daughter fiercely and known she would do anything to keep her safe and happy. Anything. Those sentiments were even stronger today.

And yet, what if she couldn't?

What if, somehow, Nick were to see Lindsay and figure out she was his daughter?

What if he tried to take Lindsay away?

Dear God.

Kristin's heart pounded crazily, even though she

knew intellectually that her fears were probably unfounded. Even if he were to see Lindsay, how could he possibly know anything?

But still...if there was even the *remotest* possibility....

Stop this, she ordered herself. *Stop this immediately! You're going to make yourself sick, and you don't have the slightest idea why he's in Green River. His reasons probably have nothing to do with you.*

"You're worried about getting married, aren't you?" Lindsay persisted. She plopped onto the bed and fastened her big dark eyes—Nick's eyes—on Kristin's face.

"A little, yes," Kristin said, relieved to have found a safe topic upon which to blame the turmoil Lindsay had somehow discerned.

"I'm gonna miss you," Lindsay said gloomily.

"I'll only be a bike ride away." Kristin sat on the bed, too. She squeezed Lindsay's shoulder in a gesture of comfort. "And you'll come and stay with us anytime you want to. Remember? You're going to have your very own room in our house."

Lindsay nodded. "It won't be the same, though."

No, Kristin thought, it wouldn't be the same. *Oh, God, I hope I'm doing the right thing....* She squeezed Lindsay's shoulder again, and for a few moments they were both lost in their own thoughts.

"You know what, Kris?" Lindsay finally said. "Mom's worried, too."

"She is? About what? Did she say something to you?" Surely not. Surely, if her mother were worried about something, she would have discussed it with

Kristin or Brooke, not Lindsay. Lindsay was only a child. Besides, from the very beginning, even though Kristin had agreed to the fiction that Lindsay was her sister, she and her parents had had an understanding. No decision concerning Lindsay would be made without Kristin's consent, and anything important happening in the family would be imparted to Lindsay by Kristin, not her mother.

"No, uh, not really." Lindsay couldn't quite meet Kristin's eyes. "I, um, just happened to hear her and Daddy talking...."

"Lindsay," Kristin said gently. "You weren't eavesdropping again, were you?"

"Well, it wasn't *really* eavesdropping...."

"Sweetie, you know listening to other people's private conversations is a very bad habit."

"I know." She picked at a loose thread on the mauve satin bedspread. Her shoulders drooped dejectedly. "But Kris, I couldn't help hearing them. They were talking awfully loud. They were mad." She looked up again, her expression troubled. "I hate it when they fight."

Kristin sighed, relenting. "I know. I do, too. So, okay, tell me. What happened?"

"Daddy said Mom is spending too much money."

"Is that all? He's always saying that," Kristin pointed out.

"This was different," Lindsay insisted. "He said he's already sold off too much stock for comfort. That's exactly what he said—*too much stock for comfort.* Kris, does that mean we're in trouble?"

Kristin tried to tamp down her irritation and anger

at her father's carelessness. Didn't he know how a comment like that could scare a child? He and her mother should be more discreet when they were having a private conversation, especially one of this nature.

"No, of course we're not in trouble," she said with more conviction than she felt. She'd had no idea her father had been selling off stock in their company. Why, ever since she was a little girl, she could remember him saying that a smart person never touched principal, and what *was* their stock if not principal?

"I don't know." Lindsay's eyes were still worried. "Daddy sounded pretty upset."

"He probably just wanted Mom to think he was upset so she'd be more careful."

"Do you really think so?"

"I really think so."

Lindsay's face brightened. "I'm glad I told you. You always make me feel better."

"You always make me feel better, too."

They smiled at each other.

"So how was the museum trip today?" Kristin asked. Lindsay's class had gone to the natural history museum in Hartford as part of the school system's enhancement program.

"It was fun."

"Oh, c'mon, you can do better than that. What did you see that you liked best?"

"The dinosaurs. They were neat."

"And what else?"

"Um, I guess the stuff about the Indians that used to live around here."

"That was always one of my favorite displays, too. Well, I'm glad you had a good time today."

"Yeah. Oh, and Kris, on the bus coming home...guess what?"

"What?"

"Kurt Hoffman asked me to be his girlfriend."

"His girlfriend! Lindsay Ann Blair, you are *much* too young to be having a boyfriend!"

"I know." Lindsay made a face. "I think Kurt is gross, anyway. He picks his nose."

Kristin burst out laughing.

After a second, Lindsay laughed, too. Then she said, "I gotta go get started on my homework. Mr. Childress gave us a *bunch* yesterday." She made another face. "And I'm going skating tomorrow afternoon, so I won't have time to do it then."

Kristin chuckled. "I guess you'd better get to work, then."

Lindsay hopped down and, giving Kristin a wave, headed off to her own room.

After she left, Kristin walked over and shut the door. Leaning against it, she closed her eyes. What a day this had been. And it wasn't over yet. Wearily she wondered what new disaster it might bring. Immediately she told herself to stop being so melodramatic.

All right, seeing Nick again had been upsetting, but perhaps there was a perfectly simple and legitimate reason for him to be in Green River—one he would soon take care of, and then he'd go back to wherever he'd come from. She had to believe that. Anything else was unthinkable. But whatever his reasons, she had no control over them or him, so worrying was counterproductive.

This business with her mother and father was a different story, though. Kristin *did* have some control over that situation. So the thing to do now was see if her mother was home and simply ask her about the conversation Lindsay had overheard.

Checking through the rear window of the upstairs hall, she saw the back of her mother's Mercedes in the open garage. Good. Meredith was home. Five minutes later, Kristin found her mother coming out of her downstairs bedroom suite.

"Hello, darling," Meredith said, looking up and smiling. As always, she was impeccably dressed in a black wool sheath and double rope of creamy pearls. Her still-firm skin glowed, and her blond hair—kept beautifully tinted by a standing monthly appointment with her hairdresser—was fashionably cut in a short, upswept style that made her look younger than her fifty-seven years. "I just got home."

"Yes, I know," Kristin said. "Um, do you think we could talk?" She lowered her voice, not wanting Milly to hear her. "Privately?"

Brow furrowing, Meredith said, "Certainly. Let's go into my office."

Years ago, when Kristin's mother had become heavily involved in charity work, she had converted a small downstairs room that overlooked the side garden and had originally been furnished as a guest bedroom into an office. Now, when she was at home, she spent most of her time there.

"All right," Kristin said.

"You go on. I just want to tell Milly to serve us our tea in there."

Kristin smiled. After her parents' first trip to England, Meredith had come home insisting that every afternoon between four and four-thirty, tea would now be served in their home. Kristin had to admit she enjoyed the ritual.

In addition to tea, which was always offered with both lemon and milk, Milly would bring them tiny sandwiches and some kind of sweet—usually thin slices of pound cake or delicious, homemade cookies. Occasionally, there would even be chess pies or Milly's cream puffs. Accordingly, the family's dinner hour had been pushed back from seven to seven-thirty.

Tonight, of course, they were all having dinner at the symphony benefit, and Kristin knew they'd be lucky to eat by nine, so tea was especially welcome.

She walked into Meredith's office and sat in one of the two flowered chintz chairs occupying one corner of the sun-filled room. The other furnishings were a low coffee table, a cherrywood desk and matching chair, a two-drawer file cabinet and a mahogany tea cart.

The desktop held a small portable computer and printer. A fax machine sat on top of the file cabinet. The walls held framed Renoir prints and the bay window afforded a colorful view of autumn roses, chrysanthemums, marigolds and nasturtiums.

It was a pleasant room, Kristin had always thought, one that suited her mother.

A few moments later, Meredith walked in. Smiling at Kristin, she sat in the other chair and crossed her legs. "Now we can talk." She looked at Kristin expectantly.

"Lindsay overheard you and Dad talking," Kristin said without preamble.

Meredith sighed. "What are we going to do with that child? I thought, after that last time, she'd learned her lesson about eavesdropping."

"You can't really blame her this time. She said you were talking so loud, she couldn't help hearing you." Kristin tried to keep her tone free of censure, but she was still irritated by her parents' lack of discretion.

"Well...maybe we *were* a bit loud," her mother conceded. "What did Lindsay say?"

"She said Dad's worried about money."

"Oh, honestly...."

"And now she's got *me* worried."

"Kristin," her mother said firmly, "this is nothing for either you or Lindsay to concern yourselves about."

"But if there *is* a problem, I feel partly responsible for it," Kristin argued. "We're spending so much money on my wedding.... Too much, I've always felt."

"This is nonsense. First of all, we are not spending too much money on your wedding. Secondly, you are not in any way responsible for your father's financial problems—if they even exist, which I seriously doubt.''

"I can't help it, Mother. It just seems like such a waste to spend so much on my wedding. I don't care about a lavish affair. I never have. I would have been happy to have a small wedding—you know that.''

"Yes, I do know that. But we have a position to uphold in this town. People expect a certain standard from us. Your father is just an old fuddy-duddy. There's plenty of money and no reason at all to worry. Besides, it's much too late to change any of the wedding plans.''

Kristin wished she felt as certain about all of this as her mother seemed to feel. Despite what she'd said to Lindsay about her father, Edmond had never stinted where his family was concerned. If he was expressing concern about finances, there must be a reason.

Still, even if there was a problem, what could Kristin do? It really was too late to change the wedding plans. The invitations had been mailed weeks ago.

While Kristin was trying to decide whether to pursue the subject, Milly entered with the tea tray. She set it on the tea cart, then pushed the cart over to where the two women sat.

"Thank you, Milly," Meredith said. "Did you call Lindsay and tell her tea was ready?''

"Yes, ma'am. She said she'll be down in a minute." Milly smiled and made her unobtrusive way out of the room as Meredith poured Kristin, and then herself, a cup.

For the next few minutes, Kristin and her mother

fixed their tea and filled their plates with today's offering of toast points spread with crab salad and lemon pound cake.

A few minutes later, Lindsay bounced into the room, and the talk turned casual. Lindsay entertained them with a hilarious story about a classmate who fell asleep in class the day before and whose friends had tacked the bottoms of his pants to the floor so that when the bell rang, and he awakened, he jumped up and his pants came down.

"He was *so* mad!" Lindsay said.

Kristin couldn't help laughing at the hapless boy.

Even Meredith chuckled, although she did say, "That was rather an unkind thing to do, wasn't it?"

"Jeff's always playing tricks on the other kids, so he deserved it," Lindsay said, unruffled by Meredith's criticism.

Kristin constantly marveled at Lindsay's confidence. She must get that from Meredith, because she certainly hadn't gotten it from Kristin. *Or maybe she got it from her father....* Kristin hurriedly shook off the unwelcome thought and turned her attention back to the conversation.

After they'd eaten, Lindsay left to go back to her homework. Kristin got up to leave, too.

"Now, darling, don't worry anymore, all right?" Meredith said. "As I told your father, if the wedding of a daughter isn't a good reason to sell off a bit of stock, I don't know what is."

Kristin gave her mother a reassuring smile. "All right. I won't worry." They hugged briefly. "I'm going up to start getting ready for tonight. Doug's picking me up at seven.''

When Kristin left, Meredith walked over to her desk. She wanted to check her calendar for the following week. With the wedding closing in on her, she knew it was going to be a busy week and would need careful planning to fit everything in.

She'd no sooner sat at the desk and picked up her daily planner when the telephone rang. She reached for the receiver. "Hello."

"Meredith? Hi, it's Amelia."

Meredith smiled. Anytime Amelia Albritton called, it could only mean juicy gossip was forthcoming. "Hi, Amelia. What's new?"

"Well..." Amelia stretched out the word. "Glenda rented Sallie Longwell's house today."

"To someone interesting, I gather."

"I'll say. Do you remember Peggy Petrillo? She used to be my cleaning lady? Well, Glenda rented the house to Peggy's son, Nick. I guess he's really successful now, and he must be loaded, because Glenda says he's driving a Lamborghini." All of this was said without pausing for a breath.

Meredith felt as if she were going to faint. Her heart knocked painfully against her rib cage.

Nick Petrillo!

No, it couldn't be.

He *couldn't* be back in Green River.

"Meredith?" Amelia was saying now. "Are you still there?"

"Yes, I...I'm still here." Meredith swallowed and battled the suffocating fear. It was all she could do to speak in a normal tone, but speak in a normal tone she must. Above all, she did not want Amelia Albritton to know how upsetting her news had been. "I knocked over a container of paper clips, and I...was trying to pick them up and listen to you at the same time."

"Oh. Well, anyway," Amelia gushed on, "isn't that a *riot?* If I remember correctly, Peggy used to work for Sallie Longwell, too. And now her *son* is renting Sallie's house! And believe me, paying a pretty penny, too, according to Glenda. It's a funny world, isn't it?"

"Yes, life is very strange sometimes," Meredith murmured.

Strange wasn't the word. *Nightmarish* was the word. *Unthinkable* was the word. Her mind continued to spin as she listened to Amelia prattle on.

What was Nick Petrillo doing in Green River?

Oh my God, does Edmond know?

Finally Amelia ran down.

"Thanks for calling, Amelia," Meredith said the first chance she got. "I really must go now, though. I haven't even started getting ready yet, and we're supposed to leave for the symphony benefit at seven."

"Me, too," Amelia said. "I'll see you there."

"Yes," Meredith said faintly.

They said their goodbyes, and Meredith slowly replaced the receiver. Her hand was trembling. Dear heaven. Nick Petrillo. Thoroughly shaken, she fought the fear clawing at her. Why had he come back? Why? And should she tell Edmond? Glancing down at her watch, she saw it was nearly five-thirty. Edmond would be home at any moment. What should she do?

I can't tell him. He'll go crazy.

As if it were yesterday, she remembered the last time Nick Petrillo's name had been spoken between her and her husband.

"He's gone," Edmond had said in tight-lipped fury. "Got on the bus this morning. McCutcheon said he put the fear of God into him."

Meredith hadn't dared say a word, even though she hadn't been in favor of Edmond's solution to the problem of Nick and Kristin, and had tried, unsuccessfully, to talk Edmond out of it, saying it somehow seemed so heartless and cruel.

"Scum," Edmond had continued. "That's all he is, scum. Putting his hands on my daughter. Thinking he could *marry* her! He'd better never show his face in this town again, or I swear, I'll kill him." He'd glared at her. "And I never want to hear his name mentioned in this house again, do you understand?"

Meredith had swallowed. "Yes, Edmond, I understand."

Oh, God.

She couldn't tell Edmond. If he were going to find out, let it be some other way.

Then a fresh fear struck her, and she gasped aloud. Kristin.

What if Kristin should happen to see Nick? Talk to him?

And the worst fear of all.

What if, somehow, Kristin should find out what *really* happened twelve years ago?

Chapter Four

"How long do you think it will take me to get telephone service?" Nick said, glancing over at Glenda.

"Not long. I'll pull a few strings."

Her smile was slow, her topaz eyes—a perfect color match for her topaz satin cocktail dress—filled with invitation and promise. Her sultry scent wafted through the close confines of the car.

"Thanks." He returned her smile, enjoying her blatant sexuality. She was the perfect companion, he decided. Beautiful, sexy, classy and best of all—a woman who knew the score. No matter how their relationship might or might not progress, he would not have to worry about messy scenes or entanglements afterward.

Nick was in a much better frame of mind than he

had been earlier. He'd been crazy to get so uptight over seeing Kristin. He'd decided his reaction was entirely due to the suddenness and unexpectedness of the encounter. But now that was out of the way, and he was back to normal and looking forward to the evening ahead.

It would be amusing to see how the upper crust of Green River society reacted to his presence, especially after they realized exactly who he was.

Although Glenda had said a tuxedo wasn't necessary, Nick hadn't wanted to be at any kind of disadvantage this evening, so he'd made a few calls and discovered that Green River now had an exclusive men's shop. He'd greased a palm or two and managed to buy a fairly decent black tux and get it altered within the space of an hour.

Money would always talk, he thought with satisfaction.

Glenda had been flatteringly appreciative, saying, "Wow," when he called for her. "I do like the way you look in a tux."

Yes, he was well pleased with himself and filled with a fine edginess—the kind that always signaled the excitement of a challenge.

As they pulled into the long circular driveway of the Green River Country Club, twilight provided a dusky violet backdrop for the sprawling white brick building and rolling landscape surrounding it. The club blazed with light, and as they queued for valet parking, Nick could see that the long French windows were open and he could hear the music of the band and the chatter of the guests who had already arrived.

The night breeze was cool and fluttered the skirt of Glenda's dress as the attendant helped her out of the low-slung car. Nick admired her long, shapely legs and again congratulated himself on his good taste and equally good luck.

Glenda slipped her hand under his arm as they climbed the broad steps and entered the gaily decorated main ballroom. This was the first time Nick had ever been inside the country club, but it looked exactly the way he'd imagined when he was a hungry-to-be-somebody kid from the wrong side of the tracks. Funny, though, he didn't feel the rush of gratification he'd thought he'd feel. That would come later, he told himself. That would come when Edmond Blair laid eyes on him for the first time.

Nick's gaze scanned the still-sparse gathering. He wondered if Kristin would be there tonight. He hoped so. He was sure her parents would be. Nothing important ever happened in Green River that they weren't a part of. He smiled. It would give him great pleasure to show all of them that they no longer had the power to keep him away from any place he chose to be.

"Let's go get a drink before we head for our table," Glenda suggested.

"You're calling the shots."

Glenda treated him to another seductive smile, leaning over to murmur into his ear. "Remember that later, okay?"

Nick grinned.

Tonight was going to be very, very interesting.

As always, Doug was prompt, ringing the front doorbell on the dot of seven. In fact, as Kristin descended the stairs to meet him, the grandfather clock in the foyer was just finishing chiming the hour. Sometimes his meticulous attention to detail and his insistence on doing everything exactly right irritated her, and she wasn't sure why.

Just before opening the door to let him in, she caught sight of herself in the foyer mirror. At the last minute, she had decided against the red chiffon dress. Instead, she now wore a dress that was part of her trousseau and intended for her honeymoon. It was the most beautiful dress she'd ever owned, and sinfully expensive. She almost hadn't bought it, but in the end had been unable to resist.

A simple silk crepe sheath in a creamy off-white, it skimmed her figure, ending a few inches above her knees. It had a wide off-the-shoulder white satin collar embroidered with golden thread and studded with hundreds of glittering golden crystals. With it, Kristin wore delicate gold lace pumps and a matching evening bag. Crystal earrings the same deep shade of gold swung from her lobes.

The colors were perfect for her, enhancing the cream and gold tones of her skin and hair and emphasizing the deep cobalt blue of her eyes.

Wearing the dress made her feel like a princess. She had needed that feeling tonight—something to chase away the shadows and fears that the earlier events of the day had produced.

Doug smiled approvingly when he saw her. "Lovely dress," he said, kissing her cheek.

"Thank you."

As always, Doug looked exactly right in his perfectly tailored tux. He was a good-looking man: tall, broad-shouldered, with nice hazel eyes and thick, light brown hair. She really couldn't fault him at all. He had an attractive smile, a pleasant personality. He was clever, even witty at times. He was always considerate and thoughtful. Always doing and saying the right thing.

If only he thrilled her, she thought sadly. If only he were thrilled *by* her. His mild reaction to her appearance tonight was typical. He liked her, and he appreciated her, but the sight of her did not fill him with joy or make his heart pound wildly. She couldn't imagine ever inciting him to passion, ever making him want her so much he would forget himself and everything else in his need.

She suppressed a sigh, telling herself once again that although there might not be any delirious highs with Doug, there would also not be any devastating lows.

Just then, her father walked into the foyer.

Doug frowned, looking at Edmond's casual attire. "Edmond, I thought you and Meredith were coming with us tonight."

Kristin's father shrugged apologetically. "Meredith's not feeling well. She said her stomach hurt, so we're going to stay home and have a quiet evening."

Kristin stared at him. Her mother had seemed perfectly fine two hours ago. And to miss the symphony benefit! Her mother was a member of the president's club and one of the symphony's staunchest backers and most successful fund-raisers.

"Well, I'm sorry to hear that," Doug said. "Be sure and give her my best."

"I will, I will," Edmond said. He smiled at Kristin, then leaned forward to kiss her cheek. "You look beautiful, my dear."

"Thank you, Daddy." Kristin was still frowning. She just couldn't believe anything short of pneumonia would keep her mother from tonight's benefit. Was there something that her father wasn't telling her? His expression seemed perfectly relaxed, though.

By the time she and Doug reached the club, Kristin had dismissed the problem of her mother and was once more focused on getting through the evening without arousing anyone's suspicion that anything was amiss.

She held Doug's arm lightly as they entered the ballroom. She smiled and greeted people while they made their leisurely way to the head table.

"Hi, Gloria. What a beautiful dress."

"Hello, Mrs. Shearer, glad to see you up and about again."

"Hi, Scott. How's that new baby?"

Then she spied Martha Sharp and her husband, Don. Martha was also on the planning committee. Kristin started to say hello and was in midsentence when, out of the corner of her eye, she saw him.

Her heart thudded painfully.

No, no, please God, no. Not here. Not tonight.

Her pleas did no good. Her eyes continued to tell her that Nick Petrillo, looking unbearably handsome and arrogant, was sitting at the head table with his head tilted toward a smiling, cat-that-ate-the-canary Glenda Carroll.

For a moment, Kristin just stood there, mesmerized. And then he looked up, and their eyes met. The expression in his was dark and challenging. She knew hers was shocked and frightened. Then, very slowly and very deliberately, he smiled.

Kristin shivered, but somehow she managed to pull herself together and finish greeting Martha, even as her mind spun with this new catastrophe. She was going to have to spend an entire evening sitting at the same table with Nick, because Glenda Carroll was the fourth member of the planning committee, and obviously, Nick was her escort. *Oh, God, this can't be happening.*

While she was still grappling with this knowledge and trying to prepare herself, Brooke, radiant in midnight blue satin evening pants and beaded maternity top, walked into the ballroom with her husband, Chandler, and headed straight for Kristin and Doug.

"Kris," Brooke breathed in breathless admiration, "you look absolutely *gorgeous!* But what happened to the red dress?"

Kristin smiled, leaning over to clutch Brooke's hand and whisper urgently in her ear. "Brooke, please sit by me, okay?"

Brooke frowned. "Sure. Is—is something wrong?"

"Yes. Very wrong."

A few moments later, the three couples moved to the head table, which was round just like the others in the room and situated in front of the bandstand. Although she tried to maneuver otherwise, Kristin ended up across the table from Nick—the worst possible place to be, she thought miserably. Now, every time she looked up, the sight of him would fill her vision.

Thank God for Brooke, who firmly sat herself on Kristin's left. Kristin knew her sister had no idea why she was upset or what was so wrong that she needed Brooke close, but she soon would. Kristin hoped Brooke was better at disguising shock than she was.

Glenda smiled gaily once everyone was seated. "Everyone, I'd like to introduce my escort, who rescued me from having to come alone, since poor Keith had to leave so unexpectedly." She turned her admiring gaze to Nick. "This is Nick Petrillo. Perhaps some of you might remember him. He used to live here in Green River." She turned to her left. "Nick, these nice people are Don and Martha Sharp, Doug Llewellyn and his fiancée, Kristin Blair, and Kristin's sister Brooke and her husband, Chandler Morris. Kristin, Brooke, and Martha are my cohorts on the planning committee for this shindig."

While the others were smiling and saying things like, "Nice to meet you," a wide-eyed Brooke reached under the table and squeezed Kristin's hand hard. Kristin returned the pressure, thankful her sister was there to give her moral support.

She didn't dare look at Brooke, though. She didn't want Nick to know how rattled she was. Bad enough she'd not been able to keep her cool earlier today and that her first sight of him tonight had revealed her surprise and dismay at his presence. She was determined that for the rest of the evening, she would be the picture of unruffled calm.

Don Sharp, a fiftyish man who was the president of the First National Bank of Green River, said, "Petrillo, Petrillo, hmmm, that name's familiar.'' He turned to his wife. "Marty, how do I...'' He broke off suddenly. After an awkward silence, he looked at Nick thoughtfully, saying, "I may have known your father.''

Nick's face revealed nothing except a cold indifference. "I'm sure you did. Everyone in Green River knew Jim Petrillo.''

"I—I'm sorry," Don said. "I didn't mean—''

"Forget it," Nick cut in. He shrugged. "It's history.''

Kristin did not want to feel anything toward Nick that was even remotely sympathetic, but she couldn't help it. She knew his indifference was pretense. Under that hard exterior beat the heart of the boy who had once held Kristin and said in a trembling voice how, if he ever had children, he would never beat them and hurt them the way his father had hurt him. He might say, "It's history," but she knew he would not have forgotten the beatings and the pain. His background had shaped him as surely as hers had shaped her.

The awkward moment passed as Nick and Don shook hands, then Martha smiled in her sweet, genuine way and said she was happy to meet Nick, and for the first time that night, a warm smile lit Nick's eyes.

"I knew your mother," Martha said. "She was a wonderful woman.''

"She still is," Nick said.

"How is she?" Martha asked.

"Doing very well.'' Nick went on to explain where his mother was living.

Kristin could hear the pride in his voice when he

talked about his mother, and she couldn't help feeling glad for him, because she was sure he was the one who had made it possible for his mother to lead the life he described. At least Kristin's father's money had done *some* good, Kristin thought, and this time she didn't feel quite as bitter.

After Martha, Doug was next in line, and he and Nick shook hands and eyed each other. Kristin knew Doug had no idea who Nick was or the importance he'd played in her life, but she wondered what Nick was thinking. She was glad Doug was someone she could be proud of, even if she didn't love him the way she should. But Nick's gaze was enigmatic, his emotions once more hidden behind closed doors.

Finally Nick's gaze swung to Kristin.

"Hello, Kristin," he said.

Brooke squeezed Kristin's hand again. Kristin smiled brightly. It was one of the hardest things she'd ever had to do, but she did it. "Hello, Nick."

"Do you two know each other?" Glenda said. Her tawny eyes were speculative.

"We're old friends," Nick said.

Kristin could feel Doug's eyes on her, and under cover of the table, Brooke squeezed her leg. For the life of her, she could not answer.

Nick's dark-eyed gaze lingered only a fraction of a second longer, then moved to Brooke and Chandler.

Finally, greetings over, the spotlight left Nick and general conversation ensued. Kristin had never felt so relieved, and she hoped the worst part of the evening was over.

She did not look at Nick again until after their waiter had poured the wine and placed baskets of warm rolls on the table. Taking a fortifying sip of her wine, she glanced across the table and was immediately sorry, because he was staring at her. Her traitorous heart gave another painful bump, and Kristin almost choked on her wine. She could feel her face heating and hurriedly turned to Brooke.

"Talk to me," she said under her breath.

"Oh, Kris, this is awful," Brooke whispered. "Just awful. What a *shock* this must have been, seeing him here tonight."

"I don't want to talk about *him*," Kristin said through gritted teeth. "Talk about something else. The weather. Anything."

Brooke shot her an apologetic look, then said, "Didn't we get a nice crowd tonight?"

The sisters continued to discuss the evening and any other subject Brooke or Kristin could drum up. Eventually, though, Kristin knew it was inexcusably rude to ignore the others at her table and she was forced to join the more general conversation.

"So what do you do, Nick?" Doug said.

"I manage a mutual fund."

"On Wall Street?"

Was it Kristin's imagination, or was Doug's voice tinged with disbelief?

Nick smiled wryly. "Yes. On Wall Street." He waited a heartbeat. "Perhaps you've heard of it. The Fiske Warburton Fund."

"The Fiske Warburton Fund!" Don exclaimed. "Why, that's the most successful new fund in years. Martha and I put a big chunk of our retirement nest egg into it last winter, and we've been tickled pink with the results."

Nick shrugged. "We've done quite well for our investors."

"He's being modest, folks," Don said, looking around the table. "What he's done for the fund is nothing short of phenomenal. I read a profile they did about him in *Money*." He turned back to Nick. "I just never connected your name with anyone I might have known." His smile was frankly admiring.

Kristin wondered if Nick would take offense at Don's remark, and was glad to see he hadn't, because she knew Don meant what he'd said as a compliment and not as a derogatory reference to Nick's background.

So Kristin had been right about Nick. He *was* very successful, and his success was due to his intelligence and skill. She had always known he had what it took to do well.

Again, she was filled with regret and sadness. *We could have had a good life together, Nick. You could have taken care of your family on your own, too. Why did you think you needed my father's money? Why couldn't you trust in yourself...in us...enough?*

"So what are you doing back in Green River?" Chandler said. "You're not leaving Wall Street, are you?"

Nick's smile was noncommittal. "No. Just some personal business."

Kristin swallowed. Personal business. What did he mean by that?

"Do you play golf?" Doug asked.

"Occasionally."

"While you're here, if you'd like a game, give me a call." Doug handed one of his business cards across the table.

Evidently, he'd decided Nick might be someone worth cultivating, Kristin thought ruefully.

As Nick took the card, his gaze met Kristin's again. Amusement sparked his eyes. Although she would have liked to look away, she lifted her chin instead. He looked away first, but not before a tiny smile tipped his lips.

It was going to be a long night, Kristin decided. A very long night.

For a few moments, conversation stopped as the waiters began serving the salads. Once everyone at their table had been served, Martha Sharp said, "I've been admiring your dress, Kristin. It's gorgeous."

Kristin smiled at the older woman. "Thank you."

"Not many women can wear white successfully," Glenda said. "You've got to have that pristine, innocent look to carry it off."

Kristin wondered if that comment was meant to be a dig, but Glenda's expression was guileless.

"Whether or not you can successfully wear white really depends on your coloring more than it does your personality," Martha said.

"I don't agree," Glenda insisted. "I think you can tell a lot about a woman's personality by the colors she wears. White is a cool, touch-me-not color." Now her smile was provocative as she turned her tawny eyes to Nick. "I, on the other hand, adore hot colors."

Nick's gaze raked Kristin. "Looks are very often deceiving."

Kristin willed herself not to blush. She wondered if anyone other than herself heard the hidden meaning behind Nick's casual-sounding comment.

"Well, I can't speak for Kristin, of course,"

Glenda drawled, "but in my case, darling, what you
see is what you get...you lucky thing...."

Nick smiled and continued to watch Kristin. "But
you're an honest woman."

There was that implication again, the same one
he'd made earlier that day, that she, Kristin, had
somehow deceived him.

"Well, Kristin's the most honest person I know,"
Brooke said loyally.

"I'm sure Nick didn't mean she wasn't," Glenda
purred.

Kristin desperately wished someone would change
the subject.

To her enormous relief, Brooke jumped in, saying,
"I have got to tell you guys what happened to me
today," and then launched into an amusing story
about being approached in the grocery store by a man
who wanted to kiss her stomach.

"He wasn't from the States," Brooke said, "and
evidently, in his land, kissing the stomach of a pregnant woman brings good luck."

"To whom?" Martha said. "The pregnant
woman?"

Brooke laughed. "I think to the person doing the
kissing. Anyway, I was so stunned, I let him. You
should have seen how the other people in the store
stared."

They all laughed.

"When are you due, Brooke?" Glenda asked.

"December 24."

"How lovely," Martha said. "A Christmas baby.
I'll bet your parents are thrilled. A first grandchild is
so very special."

Something painful pressed against Kristin's chest.

She looked down at her salad and fought for control. *A first grandchild is so very special. Oh, God, if these people only knew....* She never heard Brooke's answer. When she finally regained her composure, the conversation had moved on to football. Thank God, she thought. Surely football was a safe topic.

Chandler commented on that day's Yale football game, and soon the men were involved in a lively discussion of why the team had lost, despite the fact they'd been favored by ten points.

"Poor coaching, that's the problem," Don said.

"Oh, I don't know," Chandler said. "I think we have a tendency to blame too much on the coaches."

"I agree," Doug said. "Their biggest problem is that new running back, Breckenridge. He hasn't lived up to expectations."

"That happens all the time," Nick said. "People not living up to expectations."

Kristin knew his remark was another taunt meant for her. What she had ever done to deserve his disdain, she would never know. At this point, she didn't really care. All she wanted was to get as far away from him as she possibly could. Unfortunately, there were still a lot of hours left in the evening.

Somehow, though, she managed to endure the remainder of the dinner, even though it seemed interminable, and Nick aimed several more pointed remarks her way. She wondered if the others were aware of the undercurrents between them. She thought perhaps they were, with the possible exceptions of Doug and Chandler. She'd caught the Sharps exchanging bewildered glances a couple of times after Nick had aimed one of his well-chosen darts, and

Glenda had tilted her head and narrowed her eyes, obviously speculating.

Kristin prayed she would get through the rest of the evening without falling apart. To this end, she avoided Nick's eyes as much as possible, but even when she wasn't looking at him, she was acutely aware of him across the table. She was grateful when dinner was over and the speeches started, because then they couldn't talk.

Thank God she'd insisted Martha do the honors as mistress of ceremonies, even though Martha had wanted to share the duties among the four of them. If Kristin had had to get up there on stage and be bright and cheerful knowing that Nick's eyes were trained on her, she would have come unglued.

After the last speech, just as Kristin was about to suggest to Brooke that they visit the ladies' room before the dancing started, Martha looked at Kristin, then at Doug.

"So, you two, how are the wedding plans coming?"

Doug smiled. "That's the bride's department, so I'll defer to Kristin."

"Mother's done most of it," Kristin said. "So everything's under control. You know how thorough she is."

Martha rolled her eyes. "Don't I ever."

"Kristin and Doug are getting married in two weeks," Glenda explained, turning to Nick.

"Yes, I know. I read the engagement announcement," he said.

Kristin blinked.

"I subscribe to the *Gazette,*" he added.

Before Kristin had time to react to that statement,

Glenda said, "How about you, Nick? Have you ever been married?"

His answer was clipped. "No."

Glenda leaned closer to him, batting her eyelashes and nearly purring, "I can't *believe* you've managed to escape. Someone so handsome and successful..."

"I decided long ago that marriage is not for me," he said.

"You mean you've never even *thought* about it?" Glenda pressed. "Never even been close?"

"I was once," he said slowly, his eyes boring into Kristin's. "But she turned out to be someone quite different from the person I thought she was."

Suddenly Kristin couldn't stand another minute of his innuendo and cold looks. She stood, murmured "Excuse me, please," took her evening purse from the table and walked as fast as she could toward the ladies' room.

Once inside, she sank into one of the chairs lined up at the long vanity and tried to still her trembling hands. She was very near tears. Why? Why did he hate her so much?

"Kris?"

Kristin looked up. Her eyes met those of Brooke's in the mirror. Brooke's face was the picture of sympathy. Kristin's own face was devoid of color.

"Are you okay?" Brooke said gently, sitting down next to Kristin and putting her arm around her.

Kristin could barely speak around the lump in her throat. "What I can't understand," she whispered, "is why he hates me so. He's the one who left me, Brooke, not the other way around, yet he acts as if I'm the one who betrayed him."

Brooke bit her lip and looked down. "Listen,

Kris,'' she said haltingly, ''there's something I have to tell you. Something I should have told you years ago—'' She broke off as the door opened and two women came in, followed by three more in quick succession. ''We'll talk tomorrow, okay?''

Kristin was too upset and too worried about having to go back out and face everyone again to wonder what it was Brooke had wanted to tell her. Her only thought now was how she was going to get through the rest of the evening.

She dabbed powder on her nose and repaired her lipstick, stalling as much as she could. When she could no longer stall, she took a deep breath and said, ''Let's go face the firing squad again.''

The next hour was horrible, almost worse than the dinner had been. Although Kristin avoided being at the table when Nick was, thereby circumventing any more unpleasant remarks, she still had to watch Glenda hanging all over him, and she had to dance with Doug and others who asked her and pretend to be having a good time.

At eleven, she decided she couldn't endure another minute. She waited until Nick and Glenda were on the other side of the dance floor, then, pleading a blinding headache, she asked Doug to take her home.

''Of course, darling,'' Doug said solicitously.

Brooke hugged her goodbye, whispering, ''I'll call you in the morning.''

It took them a while to get out of the club because Kristin couldn't ignore people who wanted to say good-night or congratulate her and the committee on a job well-done. But finally they emerged into the cool night air, and Kristin trembled with relief.

Mindful of her headache, Doug didn't try to engage her in conversation on the way home. At her door, his voice was considerate. "I know you're not feeling well, so I won't come in."

"Thanks."

"Get a good night's rest."

"Yes, I will."

He tipped her chin, giving her a light, almost perfunctory kiss, then smiled down at her.

She wondered if he ever thought about the lack of passion in their relationship and if it bothered him the way it bothered her.

Doubt, stronger than any she'd had before, flooded her as she let herself into the house.

And no matter how many times she told herself she was only feeling this way because Nick's return had upset her so badly, she couldn't seem to shake the depressing thought that she was about to make the second worst mistake of her life.

Chapter Five

Meredith heard Kristin come in.

She looked at her bedside clock. The numbers glowed red. Eleven-thirty. Why had Kristin come home so early? Had something happened?

Meredith's mind whirled with the possibilities.

Did Kristin know Nick Petrillo was back? Did Glenda Carroll tell her she'd rented out the Longwell house...and to whom? Did this knowledge upset Kristin, and is that why she'd left the benefit before it was over?

Or was the explanation something simple, like Kristin was tired or just not feeling well? Or perhaps Doug was under the weather?

Meredith sighed.

If she'd gone to the benefit the way she was supposed to, she wouldn't be lying here worrying like this. She'd have known if something was wrong.

Meredith knew it was cowardly to have stayed home, but she simply hadn't been able to face the possibility that Edmond might find out about Nick while they were at the symphony benefit. She knew her husband so well, and although the majority of the time he maintained a genial facade, he had a bad temper. When crossed, he could lose control.

And when he felt his family was threatened, he tended to act first and think later.

She'd been afraid, so she'd pretended she wasn't feeling well, postponing the moment of reckoning. But it hadn't done her much good, she thought ruefully, because she'd worried all night long.

And she would continue to worry until Nick Petrillo had left Green River and gone back to wherever it was he'd come from.

Why *was* he here?

His father was dead. And his mother had moved away. So why would Nick Petrillo come back, especially if he were as successful as Amelia Albritton had intimated?

Of course, he could have other family in the area. Meredith didn't know enough about his family to know if there were brothers and sisters. Perhaps that was it. Perhaps he'd come to visit someone.

But no, that couldn't be, because if he were visiting someone, he would have had no need to rent a house. Renting a house meant he was planning to stay awhile.

Why?

The question refused to go away. Refused to let her relax enough to fall asleep. Why had Nick Petrillo come back? She listened to Edmond, breathing quietly from the next bed. She almost felt resentful that he should be sleeping so peacefully and so blissfully unaware, while she was worrying herself sick.

It was after midnight before she finally fell asleep to troubled dreams.

"Tonight was fun, wasn't it?" Glenda said to Nick.

It was a little past midnight, and they were on their way to Glenda's after leaving the symphony benefit.

"Hmm," Nick murmured noncommittally. "Fun" wasn't the way he would have described the evening.

Glenda laid her warm hand on his thigh and stroked it slowly. "But the best is yet to come...." Her hand inched up.

Nick took her hand and moved it back to her lap. To take the sting out of his action, he forced a lightness into his voice that he did not feel. "Behave yourself, Glenda. I'm driving."

Her answering chuckle said she'd taken no offense. "Not for long," she drawled.

It was obvious to Nick that Glenda was counting on him joining her in her bed tonight. Although he was sure making love to her would be a very diverting way to spend the next couple of hours, he had absolutely no desire to do so.

The trouble was, he did not feel the triumph or satisfaction he would have expected to feel after tonight's encounter with Kristin and her friends. He'd intended to show them he was their equal, that he could hold his own in theirs or any other company.

Instead, he couldn't rid himself of the feeling he'd behaved in a way no gentleman ever would. He had treated Kristin badly, saying things to her that barely missed being insults.

The knowledge shamed him.

"How did you and Kristin Blair get to be friends?"

The question startled him, coming as it did while Kristin was on his mind, and a few seconds went by before he was collected enough to answer. "We were never really friends," he said quietly.

"But you said—"

"I know what I said, Glenda." Realizing he'd answered curtly, he softened his voice. Man, that's all he had to do. Get Glenda's curiosity aroused even more than it was. Besides, she didn't deserve to be snapped at. She'd done nothing wrong. "I met Kristin years ago...when we were both kids. We had a mutual friend, that's all."

"Really? I kind of got the idea there might have been bad blood between the two of you."

Although he was looking straight ahead, he could feel Glenda's eyes on him. "You thought wrong."

Now it was her turn to say, "Hmm."

Nick knew she was unconvinced. He started to say something else, then abruptly stopped as he remembered the first and most important rule of verbal sparring. *Never explain, never defend.*

She said nothing more, and a few minutes later he pulled into Glenda's driveway and cut the engine.

She waited for him to walk around to her side of the car and help her out. As he did, she pressed her body against his briefly before taking his hand and leading him around to the back door. She smiled up at him expectantly as she unlocked the door.

"Thanks for inviting me tonight," Nick said once the door was open. "I enjoyed it."

"The night's only just begun," she purred, putting her arms around his waist and lifting her face.

He held her loosely. "Not for me." He kept his voice light. "Sorry, but it's been a long day, and I'm bushed." He dropped a quick kiss on her upturned lips. "Thanks again."

"But Nick," she protested as he released her. "I—"

"Really, Glenda," he interrupted firmly. "I'm not fit company."

He was afraid she might continue to try to persuade him to stay, but after a moment, she simply sighed and said, "I'm not going to see you again, am I?"

He considered hedging, then decided she deserved honesty. "I'm sorry."

She shrugged. "Don't be. Win some, lose some, that's my motto. 'Night, Nick. Enjoy your stay in Green River. And if you change your mind, you know where to find me."

Kristin had a hard time falling asleep. Her mind had been in too much turmoil. As a result, she awakened late on Sunday morning, and the family had already gone to church. She was grateful. She wasn't in the mood to face anyone or to answer questions about the symphony benefit.

If her mother had gone to church, she must be feeling better this morning, Kristin reflected as she descended the stairs and headed for the kitchen. She hoped there was coffee. Sunday was Milly's day off and she always went to her daughter's home for the day, but surely Kristin's mother had made a pot. Yes, it had been left on the warmer, and there was enough for a couple of cups.

Kristin gratefully poured herself a mugful and had just taken her first sip when the phone rang.

"Kris? Oh, good. You're up." It was Brooke. "How are you feeling today?"

Kristin grimaced. "I've had better days."

"Oh, Kris." Brooke's voice was filled with sympathy. "It must have been a terrible shock to see Nick there last night. Had you any idea?"

"I knew he was in town. I ran into him earlier in the day. But I didn't know he would be there last night." Kristin shuddered. She wished she could erase the whole of yesterday from her memory.

"Oh, Kris," Brooke said again.

"It's okay. I survived."

"Um, about last night... You know how I said there was something I had to tell you?"

Kristin frowned. She had forgotten. "Yes...."

"Well, it's really important. And I don't want to talk over there. Have you eaten breakfast yet?"

"No."

"Then why don't you come over here, and I'll fix us some brunch and we can talk?"

"All right. But now you've got me worried. Is everything okay?"

"*I'm* fine, if that's what you mean. It's nothing like that. Just that there's something I need to discuss with you."

"All right. I'll come over. But it'll be at least an hour before I can get there. I just got up, and I've got to shower and dress." As she walked back upstairs to get ready, she decided it might be a good thing to listen to Brooke's problems for a while. Maybe that way, Kristin could stop thinking about her own.

An hour and ten minutes later, Kristin pulled into the circular drive of the two-story white frame Colonial home that was only six blocks away from the house she would occupy with Doug after they were married. Brooke and Chandler had bought their house two years earlier, just before their own wedding.

Kristin liked the house. It suited Brooke and Chandler, who were as upbeat and cheerful a couple as anyone would ever want to meet. As Kristin walked to the front door, she admired the well-tended beds of pansies and chrysanthemums.

She liked the interior of the house, too, which reflected Brooke's eclectic taste in furnishings. The rooms were just as likely to contain a lacquered Chinese trunk or an Oriental screen festooned with gossamer scarves as the more traditional-style sofas and tables and chairs.

Brooke had set the small glass-topped table in the

sunroom for their brunch. Seeing only two place settings, Kristin said, "Isn't Chandler joining us?"

"No, he's playing golf this morning." Brooke inclined her head toward a wicker table laden with a silver coffee service. "Help yourself. I'll go get the rest of the food."

A few minutes later, Brooke carried in plates filled with cantaloupe, fresh sliced strawberries and fluffy mushroom omelettes. Kristin relaxed for the first time since entering the ballroom of the country club the night before. For a while, the sisters ate in silence.

Finally Brooke laid her fork down and sat back with a sigh. A few moments went by while she seemed to collect her thoughts. "Kris? Last night...when you said you didn't understand why Nick acted as if you'd done something wrong...?"

"Yes," Kristin said, immediately on guard.

Brooke's eyes were troubled. "I—I know why."

"*You* know why?"

"Yes. I can't tell you how bad I feel about this. I've felt bad about it for a long time. And I've wanted to tell you about it for a long time, too, but I've..." She swallowed. She could hardly meet Kristin's eyes. "I've been too cowardly."

"What in the world are you talking about?"

"Remember how, the night before you and Nick were going to run away together, I walked in on you and discovered you packing a suitcase?"

"Yes."

"And how you ended up confiding in me and swearing me to secrecy?"

All Kristin could do was nod.

"Well, the next day, I...oh, God, Kris. I let something slip that made Mom suspicious. I didn't mean to, but I was only thirteen. Way too young for such an important secret." Her eyes implored Kristin to understand. "Mom badgered me until she got the whole story out of me."

Kristin stared at her sister. "You...you told Mom I was planning to run away with Nick?"

Brooke nodded. "Yes. I didn't want to, but I was scared, and you know how Mom is. She wouldn't let it go. She told me it was for the best, that she needed to know so she could protect you."

"*Protect* me?"

"Yes."

Kristin's mind spun. Her parents had known what she was planning. They'd known! "What...what did they do?"

"Daddy had Nick arrested."

"Oh my God..."

"Yes, Daddy got Sheriff McCutcheon to throw Nick in jail on some kind of trumped-up charge, and then Daddy went to see Nick. He gave him a note that you'd supposedly written."

Kristin listened in shock as Brooke explained that their mother had written the note and that it told Nick Kristin had changed her mind, that she could never marry someone like him, that she was going to Europe with her family and never wanted to see him again.

She could never marry someone like him....

Of all the things they could have said, Kristin

couldn't imagine anything that could hurt Nick more.

"And that's not all," Brooke continued. "Daddy wrote a check out to Nick and had Mr. Evans at the bank stamp the back of it so it would look as if Nick had cashed it."

Kristin put her hand over her mouth and stared at her sister. Dear God. That was the check her father had shown her. The check she thought Nick had chosen in preference to her.

No wonder Nick hated her. He thought she'd thrown him over because he wasn't good enough for her. And she...she had thought he'd thrown her over for money.

Deceived.

Both of them.

Made to believe the other had betrayed them.

And all of it—the whole treacherous scheme—was conceived and executed by her parents.

Kristin could hardly take it in. All these years. All the pain. Lindsay. Everything she and Nick had lost. All of it. The result of her parents' interference.

"Kris, I'm sorry," Brooke said sadly. "I swear to you, I didn't know what Mom and Dad were going to do. If I had, I never would have told Mom anything. In fact, I didn't know for a long time what they *had* done. I only knew that Nick was gone and you were so unhappy. And then, of course, I knew about Lindsay." She fiddled with her napkin. "I finally put it all together years later when I remembered things Mom and Dad said that night. A couple of years ago, I just came out and asked Mom about it, and she admitted everything."

Blindly, Kristin stood. There was a huge knot in her chest. "I—I have to go. I have to think."

Brooke didn't try to stop her. But she did follow Kristin outside. "Are you sure you're okay?" she said as Kristin climbed into her car.

Kristin nodded, but she'd never felt less okay in her life. Still, the habits of a lifetime were hard to break, so she tried to reassure Brooke. Then, as she had so many other times when she was upset or troubled, she headed for Primrose Hill.

Meredith was grateful when the service was over. It was too much of a strain, being there at the church, surrounded by friends, and having to keep up the pretense of having had some kind of twenty-four-hour bug that had kept her from the benefit the night before.

Only a few more minutes, she thought as she and Edmond and Lindsay exited St. Paul's, where they'd been members all of their lives. "Lovely service, Reverend Lewis," she said with a bright smile.

She kept the smile pasted on, greeting people right and left. Just as she thought they were going to escape without any long conversations, Silas Guthrie, the treasurer and chief financial officer of Edmond's company, waved at Edmond.

Meredith groaned inwardly. She liked Silas, but he had a tendency to be long-winded and boring. He also had a tendency to be gloomy. She simply wasn't in the mood for any of those traits this morning.

Sure enough, even though she tugged at Edmond's arm and told him she was still feeling a bit peaked and really wanted to go home, Silas refused to take the hint. He pulled Edmond off on the fringes of the departing crowd, and Meredith—with a bored Lindsay standing nearby—was forced to endure a lengthy description of Janet Stillwater's latest operation. Throughout, Meredith kept one eye on her husband's back.

Finally, Edmond and Silas parted. Meredith said a hurried goodbye to Janet and beckoned to Lindsay, who was now in animated conversation with Dawn Seebert, one of her best friends. "Lindsay, darling, come on, we're going now."

Lindsay and Dawn walked over. "Dawn wants me to come over to her house. Can I?"

"May I?" Meredith corrected automatically.

Lindsay and Dawn exchanged grins. "May I?" Lindsay said.

"How will you get home?"

"My mom will drive her home," Dawn, a cute little redhead, said.

Meredith gave her permission happily, thinking that now she could talk to Edmond freely about whatever it was that had Silas Guthrie so concerned.

"What was *that* all about?" she said once they were in the Cadillac and bound for home.

"Silas is worried," Edmond said. "A big block of stock was sold to an investor on Friday, and Silas is afraid of a corporate raider because he's never heard of this company."

"Silas is an old woman," Meredith said.

"Maybe he is, but this time he may be right to be worried. And now he's got me worried, too."

"But Edmond, what's wrong with a company buying stock in Blair Manufacturing? I mean, I would think you'd be concerned if people *didn't* want our stock."

"Normally, nothing, but I've sold off so much stock that I'm no longer the majority shareholder. Silas is worried about the upcoming shareholders' meeting."

"I still don't understand why. Has this company, whoever they are, bought a *majority* of the stock? Is that what you're saying?"

"We don't know."

"How could you not know?" She was honestly bewildered.

"Because," Edmond said none too patiently, "we have no way of finding out if this company is related in any way to other companies that have bought stock in the past. And we won't know until they make their move. Although Silas *did* say he was going to do some intensive digging to try to get more information."

"You mean you think the same person or group of people has been buying stock in the names of different companies? To throw you off track?"

"Yes, that's what we're afraid of."

Meredith bit her lip. Something else to worry about. Now there was no way she was going to tell Edmond about Nick Petrillo's return, not on top of this. And maybe she'd been worrying about Nick Petrillo for nothing, anyway. Maybe his return to Green River had no significance and maybe he would be long gone before Edmond ever knew he'd been there.

That's it. She would think positively and not borrow trouble. She patted Edmond's leg. "Don't worry, darling. It'll all work out all right. I'm sure of it. Let's not let silly old Silas spoil Kristin's wedding or anything else."

Edmond nodded, but the lines of strain remained.

Just in case, Meredith decided perhaps she'd better pray.

It was after one before Kristin left Primrose Hill. After thinking and thinking, she'd finally decided what she had to do. She had to see Nick.

She drove straight to the Longwell home. She prayed Nick would be there. Now that she'd made up her mind to talk to him, she didn't want to wait. This would be hard enough. She just wanted to get it over with.

A red Lamborghini with New York plates was parked in the driveway. He was there.

Kristin's heart beat faster. Pulling in behind the sports car, she took several deep breaths for courage, then switched off the ignition.

Then slowly she climbed out of her car, walked to the door and pressed the doorbell.

Nick had just finished showering and was halfway dressed when the doorbell rang. Hurriedly shrugging into a black knit turtleneck and jeans, he ran a comb through his wet hair and shoved his feet into loafers, then headed for the front door.

Shock radiated through him when he saw Kristin standing on the doorstep. "Kristin. Hello," he said, hoping he'd covered his surprise. What was she doing there?

"Hello, Nick."

He wondered if seeing her would always have this effect, like someone had knocked the wind out of him.

"I have to talk to you," she said. "May I come in?"

"Sure." He stood back, holding the door open so she could enter. She was wearing jeans and a pale pink sweater under a navy wool blazer, and he thought how no matter what she put on, she looked classy. Of course, the fact that the jeans and blazer were designer and the sweater was probably cashmere didn't hurt. "Let's go into the living room."

"All right."

Following her, he caught a whiff of the light, flowery fragrance she wore, and something tightened in his groin. Irritated with himself, he motioned toward the burgundy sectional sofa that took up a major portion of the room and said, "Have a seat," more brusquely than normal.

She perched on the end of the sofa. The way she clasped her hands together tightly, her whole body language, told him she was agitated.

Nick had learned patience long ago. He'd also learned that in any kind of adversarial relationship, you waited for the opponent to make the first move. He walked to the fireplace, propped one arm on the mantel and waited for her to say whatever it was she'd come to say.

"I don't know where to start," she said. She

looked down, then slowly raised her eyes to meet his. "I—I learned something today, something I think you need to know."

Still he said nothing.

"My sister...Brooke? She told me what happened to you that night...the night you and I were going to go away together."

"What do you mean?"

"She said you were arrested."

"Are you saying you didn't know I'd been arrested?"

"That's right. I never knew until today. I would have come to see you if I'd known."

He listened, first in disbelief, then in mounting anger, as she explained exactly how her parents had thwarted their elopement plans—how her mother had faked the note to Nick, how her father had shown her a "canceled" check supposedly cashed by Nick. Her voice faltered several times, but she kept going. "They lied to both of us," she finished quietly.

For a moment, he just stared at her. "How could you believe I'd take money from your father?" he finally demanded furiously.

"Well, how could *you* believe I wouldn't come to you in jail? Besides, I didn't want to believe it, but I saw the canceled check. And you never called me again. What was I *supposed* to think?" Her eyes brimmed with tears.

He pushed back the wave of sympathy her tears elicited. The fact was, she hadn't trusted him or loved him enough to believe in him. "I called you," he said tightly. "Your housekeeper said you'd gone to Europe."

"But that was *days* later!"

"I was kept locked up for days. I *couldn't* call you sooner. What's *your* excuse?"

"I tried to call you," she said, "the very next day, but no one answered the phone." Her lower lip trembled. "And then my father showed me the check and said you'd gone. Oh, Nick, I'm so sorry. So sorry for…everything."

Because his emotions were so chaotic and he needed time to think, he fell back into his tough-guy mode, a mode that had served him well anytime he felt vulnerable. "It was a long time ago." His tone was matter of fact, but inside he was seething with rage and renewed pain and frustration.

Damn Edmond Blair!

Damn his lying hide to hell.

All the years of dreaming about Kristin, of repressing the need inside him, of denying the part of him that wanted a loving connection with a woman, rose up to engulf Nick in a rage so fierce, he thought he might burst with it.

In that moment, he knew he'd been right to come back. Nothing on earth would stop him now. He would wrest control of Blair Manufacturing from her scheming father if it was the last thing he ever did. He shrugged. "It no longer matters." He was holding on to his control by the slimmest of threads.

For a long moment, she was silent. The mantel clock ticked loudly as the seconds passed. Then, eyes still troubled, she slowly stood. "All right. I won't take up any more of your time. I just thought you should know.''

"Yes. Thank you.''

They might have been strangers, their voices were so polite, so devoid of emotion.

Briefly, her gaze met his again. "Goodbye, Nick.''

"Goodbye.''

Something twisted inside him as she walked out of the room, and the enormity of everything he had once had and lost sank in.

Long after she was gone, Nick stood by the window, staring out and seeing nothing.

Chapter Six

Kristin drove home blindly. She felt battered and completely devastated by the morning's events. She wasn't sure what she had expected from Nick, but the reaction she'd gotten wasn't it, especially when he'd said none of what had happened twelve years ago mattered now.

Of course it mattered now, she'd wanted to cry. It mattered because her parents' manipulation and deceit had stolen something precious from both of them and changed the course of their lives.

And not just *their* lives.

It had also changed Lindsay's life.

Of course, he doesn't know about Lindsay, does he?

Kristin's lip trembled.

Should she have told Nick about Lindsay? He was

Lindsay's father. Didn't he have a right to know he had a child? She had never thought so before, but until this morning, she had believed he'd deserted her.

Now everything had changed.

He *hadn't* deserted her. He'd been lied to the same way she had been and then he'd been forced to leave town. Nothing that had happened was his fault. Yet he'd paid an even steeper price than Kristin had paid. At least she'd had Lindsay.

So, yes, she should tell him.

And yet, how could she, when telling him would tear apart so many lives—Lindsay's most of all?

Lindsay was happy and secure. She loved Kristin's parents, and they loved her. And no matter how angry with her father Kristin was, she couldn't deny he had been a wonderful parent to Lindsay. He had many things to answer for—and Kristin certainly intended to confront him over them—but he had never treated Lindsay as anything other than a beloved youngest daughter.

And what would telling Nick accomplish, anyway? The knowledge that he had a child who had been hidden from him all these years would probably only further incense and embitter him. For embittered he was, no matter how he'd pretended otherwise.

Please, God, help me....

Her thoughts whirled, but no matter how she looked at the situation, no matter how much she might want to, she knew she couldn't tell Nick about Lindsay. She was too afraid of what Nick would do with the knowledge.

She simply couldn't take that chance.

No, the only option open to her was to continue to keep her secret and pray that Nick would leave Green River soon.

When Kristin pulled into the driveway, both her parents' cars were visible in the open garage. Good. She could talk to them right now. This wouldn't be pleasant, but that was all the more reason to get it over with. As she climbed out of the car and walked into the house, she promised herself that no matter what was said, she would try to remain calm. She'd learned long ago that anytime she lost her temper, she usually lost whatever battle it was she was fighting. Besides, she hated angry confrontations and would usually do anything to avoid them.

But most important of all, she did not want Lindsay to get wind of trouble between Kristin and her parents. And if they had a knock-down-drag-out, full-fledged fight, there'd be no way Lindsay *wouldn't* get wind of it.

"Well, hello, darling. I wondered where you'd gone," Meredith said, as Kristin entered the dining room where it looked as if her parents had just sat down to lunch.

Edmond looked up from the morning paper and smiled.

"Brooke asked me to brunch," Kristin said. She looked around. "Where's Lindsay?"

"Dawn invited her over after church," Meredith said. She ground fresh pepper onto her chicken salad. "She should be home soon."

"Good," Kristin said. "I'm glad she's not here because there's something I wanted to talk to you about." She looked at her father, but he'd buried his nose in the newspaper again. "You, too, Dad."

"Hmm?" Her father lowered the paper. "What about me?"

"I said, I need to talk to you and Mother."

Both parents looked at her expectantly.

Kristin pulled out a chair and sat down. She took a deep breath and plunged in. "Nick Petrillo has come back to Green River."

If she had dropped a bomb into the room, she couldn't have gotten a more profound reaction. Her mother's face drained of color and the fork she held in her hand clattered to her plate.

Her father, in contrast, turned red and glowered at Kristin with thunder in his eyes. "What the hell is he doing here? Has he contacted you?" he said through clenched teeth.

"No. I ran into him yesterday, quite by accident. And then, last night, I saw him again. He came to the symphony benefit as Glenda Carroll's escort, so we sat at the same table all evening."

Meredith sucked in her breath. Her gaze was filled with fear as it darted to Kristin's father, then back to Kristin.

Kristin's father looked as if he were going to explode.

"It was obvious to me, and probably to others, that Nick dislikes me intensely," Kristin pressed on, determined to get everything out in the open, "because he said some things that were—"

"What things?" her father shouted, jumping up. "Why, I'll smash that no-good lowlife's face in if he dares to say one more word to you!"

"Daddy," Kristin said quietly, even though her pulse was racing, "please. Sit down. Let me finish."

Meredith reached over to pat her husband's hand as, still grumbling, he sank back into his chair.

"The only reason I told you about him making some remarks is that his attitude not only upset me, it puzzled me. I just couldn't understand why he was acting as if I was the one who had done something to him, when I'd always felt it was the other way around. I said as much to Brooke, and..." Kristin paused, looking from one parent to the other. "She ended by confessing everything that happened twelve years ago."

"Wh-what do you mean?" Meredith said.

Kristin met her father's eyes. "I think you both know what I mean." As the seconds passed and neither parent said anything, her gaze swung to Meredith. "Brooke told me about the note you wrote to Nick and how you signed my name to it, Mother."

Her mother looked miserable and could hardly meet Kristin's eyes.

Kristin slowly turned back to her father. "She also told me about you having Nick arrested and thrown in jail and about the check you faked, Daddy."

"I knew this would happen someday. I just knew it," Meredith said. "I told you, Edmond—"

"Shut up, Meredith," Edmond said.

"Why did you do it, Daddy? Why did you lie to me and ruin my life?" All of Kristin's attempts to be calm and deal quietly with the issue evaporated, and her voice trembled as she fought hurt and angry tears.

"I did not ruin your life," he said. "I saved your life, and instead of accusing me of doing something wrong, you should be thanking me."

"*Thanking* you?"

"Yes, thanking me. Nick Petrillo is bad news. Always has been. Always will be. I told you once, and I'll say it again. He's trash."

"He's not trash," Kristin said. "He's made a tremendous success of himself. You should see the way he looks and the car he drives. It's obvious he's making a lot of money. And the other night, he told Doug he manages a mutual fund, and Doug recognized it. He and Don Sharp both said it's a hugely successful one. In fact, Don said he and Martha had put a big chunk of money in that fund, mainly because Nick has done such a fantastic job with it."

"Just because he's made money doesn't change what he is underneath," Edmond said scornfully. "Money doesn't buy class. Look at his family. No daughter of mine was going to marry into a family like that."

"Whether or not I married Nick was *my* decision to make, not yours. I *loved* him!"

"Love! What did you know about love? You were only seventeen, still a child. It was my responsibility to protect you," Edmond said implacably. He shook his head. "I did the right thing, what any father would do who cared about his daughter. And I'm not sorry."

"Well, you should be. In fact, you should be ashamed! What you did was terrible. Unforgivable!"

Her father slammed his hand down on the table, and his water glass overturned, spraying water everywhere. They all ignored it. "Listen to me, young lady. You're the one who did something she should be ashamed of. And you know very well what the result was."

"Oh, Edmond," her mother said.

Kristin stared at him. This was the first time he'd ever held the subject of Lindsay over her head. "Yes," she said with as much dignity as she could muster. "I do. The result was a loving and lovely child whom I love more than anyone in the world. And whom I thought you loved, too."

"Now you know damn well I love that child as much, more even, than I love you and your sister. Hell, she's my *granddaughter!* That is not the point."

"I'm not sure you know what the point is." Kristin shook her head. She felt exhausted and very, very tired. It was useless. Her father would never admit any wrongdoing. She should have known better than to have thought anything else.

"Kristin," her mother said softly. "Please..."

"Please, what, Mother?" Kristin said bleakly. "Just forget what you and Daddy did? Just blithely put it out of my mind and pretend this never happened? That my parents *didn't* lie to me and trick me and drive away the man I loved and deprive my daughter of the chance to know her father? And me—deprive me of the chance to acknowledge my child to the world?''

Her mother's eyes filled with tears.

''It was all so very long ago,'' she said. ''And you *were* so very young. Oh, God. I know it was wrong, and I'm sorry we deceived you, darling, but we really did believe we were doing the right thing. I—I never realized you felt this way. I honestly thought you were happy all these—''

''Enough!'' said Kristin's father, slapping the table again and making the cutlery bounce. ''Of course she's been happy. Why wouldn't she be happy? I don't want to hear another word on this subject. From either one of you! Do you hear me?'' He glared at his wife. ''None of this matters anymore, anyway, so I don't know why you're both so hysterical. Kristin is marrying Doug in two weeks. End of story.''

Kristin wondered what her father would think if he knew he had echoed almost the exact words Nick had used, saying none of this mattered any longer. That sentiment seemed to be the belief of everyone except her.

She knew she could continue to argue with her father. She could shout and cry and tell him she'd never forgive him. She could say all kinds of hurtful things to him. But what was the point? What would further accusations accomplish? Would they change anything? Improve anything?

No, she thought sadly.

The only thing she would accomplish would be to upset everyone even more than they were upset now. If Kristin only had herself to think of, maybe she would force the issue further, but she didn't just have herself.

She had Lindsay.

So Kristin nodded wearily and rose, saying, "Fine. We won't speak of it again. I'm going upstairs. I don't feel well. I want to lie down." She couldn't bring herself to say goodbye or anything else conciliatory. Her emotions were still too raw. Not looking at either of her parents, she walked out of the room and slowly headed for the stairs.

Just as she placed her foot on the bottom stair, she saw a flash of red on the landing, but by the time she reached the top, the hall was empty. Oh, God. Was that Lindsay? Had she come home while Kristin and her parents had been arguing?

Suddenly Kristin's heart began to pound. Terror flooded her. What had they said? Dear heaven, what had they said?

Kristin reached the upstairs landing. Lindsay's door was closed. Whispering a silent prayer, Kristin knocked softly. All she heard in return was a muffled sound.

"Lindsay?" Kristin opened the door.

Lindsay, wearing a red blouse, was sitting on her bed. She looked at Kristin. "Hi."

Her dark eyes—so like Nick's, thought Kristin with a pang—were definitely troubled. "Hi," said Kristin softly, walking over to the bed and sitting down. "I thought you were at Dawn's house."

"I was."

"When did you get home?" *Please, please, God, don't let her have heard anything I can't explain.*

her father were right. If only none of it mattered anymore.

Unfortunately for her, it did matter.

It mattered a lot because it destroyed all of her
beliefs about her life and her choices and made her
question if there was anything at all she could have
done differently. And it had finally made her face the
fact that she and her family had deprived Lindsay
and Nick of the right to know each other.

Oh, God, what a tangled mess their lives were—
and all because two kids had once fallen in love.

Nick had to work off his rage somehow, so he
drove—much faster than was sensible or safe—to the
gym he'd noticed yesterday.

Fifty dollars bought him a membership.

For the next couple of hours, he drove himself
relentlessly, methodically going from one machine to
the next until he'd used every one. He ended up on
the treadmill where he ran ten miles before stopping.
Finally he headed for the steam room followed by
the showers.

All the while, Kristin's revelations turned round
and round in his head. Nothing was happening the
way he'd envisioned it. He'd thought he would come
to Green River, fling his success in the faces of the
townsfolk who'd doubted him—especially those
who'd had a hand in running him out of town—exact
his revenge on Edmond Blair and Kristin, and then
return to Manhattan triumphant and vindicated.

Now, thinking about the sadness in Kristin's eyes,

for the first time, doubt seeped in and he wondered if he was doing the right thing.

Yet he must be.

After all, what had really changed? Edmond Blair was even more of a bastard than Nick had thought he was to begin with. So why was he hesitating, for even a second?

Edmond Blair deserved everything he was going to get. And then some.

By the time Nick returned to the Longwell house, he had put aside the last lingering doubts and was once more convinced that only until Kristin's father had been made to pay would the older man understand that no one had the right to mess around with other people's lives.

Meredith had a hard time sleeping. She had never felt so guilty and so wrong about anything in her life. She and Edmond had had no right to do what they'd done to Kristin. Meredith had always known it; she just hadn't wanted to face it.

Meredith couldn't even find it in her heart to be angry with Brooke, even though she wished Brooke hadn't told Kristin. Not because she wanted to protect herself or Edmond. No, they deserved Kristin's censure.

She wished Brooke hadn't told Kristin because she knew Kristin was hurt—needlessly, Meredith felt. After all, what was done was done. Nothing could change the facts.

Because her night was so restless, when she awakened on Monday morning, Meredith had a headache.

For a while, she considered calling the resale shop sponsored by three local churches and begging off her regular Monday-morning volunteer job of manning the store, but her sense of duty and responsibility won out over her need to pamper herself, and she got up.

Forty minutes later, showered and dressed in trim navy slacks and matching jacket worn over a white sweater, she walked into the dining room to find that Kristin and Lindsay were already there eating their breakfast.

"Good morning, sweetie." Meredith dropped a kiss on the top of Lindsay's head.

Lindsay smiled up at her. Her "G'mornin', Mommy" was muffled by a mouth full of Cheerios.

Meredith refrained from telling Lindsay not to talk with her mouth full. Instead, she took a deep breath, then slowly met Kristin's gaze. "Good morning, darling." She injected into her voice a note of cheerfulness that she did not feel.

Kristin's eyes were cool as she returned Meredith's greeting.

Meredith walked to the sideboard where she poured herself a cup of coffee. She dawdled over adding nondairy creamer and a packet of sweetener, delaying the moment when she would have to face that cool gaze once more. But finally, she could delay no longer, and she walked to her place at the table and sat down. A few minutes later, Milly brought in Meredith's standard breakfast: half a grapefruit and a toasted bagel spread with nonfat cheese and raspberry jam.

The three of them ate in silence for a few minutes, then, in an effort to make the morning seem as normal as possible, Meredith looked at Kristin and said, "It looks like a lovely day. Do you have anything special planned for the morning?"

"I'm supposed to meet with the landscaper."

Meredith waited, but when Kristin didn't elaborate, she said, "I haven't seen the house since you picked out the carpeting and wallpaper and Doug moved in."

"It turned out well" was Kristin's clipped reply.

Meredith sipped at her coffee and eyed her oldest daughter over the rim of the cup. She had hoped Kristin would be in a forgiving mood this morning, but obviously it was going to take a while for them to get back to their old relationship, because if Kristin was this cool in front of Lindsay, she must still be very angry.

Maybe you never will get back to your old relationship.

The thought hurt.

Meredith suddenly wished Lindsay wasn't there. She would have liked to apologize to Kristin again, maybe get up and go over to her and give her a hug. Something, anything, really, to banish the undercurrent of strain permeating the room.

She sighed and took a bite of her bagel and tried to think of something else to say.

A few moments later, Kristin wiped her mouth and put down her napkin. She got up, avoiding Meredith's eyes. "Have a good day, honey," she said to Lindsay. "You, too, Mother. I'll see you both later."

She disappeared upstairs.

Meredith finished her breakfast, saw Lindsay off to the school bus, debated whether she should go upstairs and try to talk to Kristin again, then thought perhaps it might be better to give Kristin the day to cool down. Maybe by tonight, she'd be in a more receptive frame of mind. And if she wasn't, maybe Meredith would wait a couple of days, then reintroduce the subject.

Sooner or later, despite Edmond's admonition about dropping the subject, Meredith knew she and Kristin would have to discuss it again. They simply could not leave things the way they were.

Kristin knew her mother wanted to smooth things over between them, but she wasn't in the mood to pretend. Once she gained the privacy of her room, she headed straight for the telephone and dialed Brooke's number.

"Oh, Kris, I'm *so* glad you called," Brooke said. "I worried about you all day yesterday. Are you okay?"

"More or less. Listen, can I come over?"

"Sure. Did you talk to Mom and Dad?"

"Yes."

"Oh, God. Yes, come on over. And hurry, will you?"

When Kristin arrived at Brooke's, the sisters took one look at each other and then they were hugging tightly.

"I'm so sorry, Kris," Brooke whispered.

"It wasn't your fault."

"But I feel so guilty."

"I don't want you to feel guilty. I didn't come over here to make you feel bad. I just wanted to tell you about everything that happened after I left here yesterday."

"Why don't we go in the sunroom? I made a pot of coffee and it's waiting."

"All right."

Once they were settled with their coffee, Kristin said, "I went to see Nick yesterday."

Brooke's eyes widened. "Oh, wow. Did you tell him what I'd told you?"

"Yes."

"What did he say?"

Kristin relayed the conversation as accurately as she remembered, ending with, "So you can see how bitter he is, even though he said it no longer mattered."

"I think you're right. He was just covering up his emotions. That's what men do." She paused, giving Kristin a thoughtful look. "Maybe he wants you back."

"I don't *think* so."

"Don't be so sure."

"No, Brooke, he hates me. He blames me for what happened just as much as he blames Daddy."

"Maybe I shouldn't have told you about—"

"You did the right thing," Kristin said, breaking in. "It was time for the truth. I'm very glad you told me."

"Are you, Kris?"

"Yes."

"Well, c'mon, tell me about Mom and Dad. What did they say when you told them you knew about their role in all of this?"

Kristin swallowed. The hurt she'd felt yesterday was muted today, but there was a dull ache around her heart she wasn't sure would ever completely disappear. She had always trusted her parents implicitly. Now she wasn't sure she would ever trust them again.

"Mom feels bad. She apologized. But Dad refused to admit he'd done anything wrong. In fact, he was furious. Although most of his anger was directed toward Nick. He really hates Nick."

Silence fell between them. For a long moment, neither spoke. Then Brooke said softly, "You've never gotten over Nick, have you?"

Kristin sighed. "No. I thought I had, but seeing him again...I don't know...it awakened all the old feelings." She smiled sadly. "Most people would probably think I'm crazy, because he's so changed. But the other night, at the benefit, there were glimmers of the old Nick. The way he looked when he talked about his mother, for instance. I just have this feeling that underneath that hard exterior, the Nick I knew and loved is still there."

Brooke sighed, too. "What are you going to do?"

"What *can* I do?"

"Well, for starters, you could tell him about Lindsay."

Kristin shook her head. "No. I can't." She went on to explain her reasoning. "Don't you think I'm right?"

"I don't know." Brooke bit her lip. "What about Doug?"

Kristin moaned. "Oh, God. I haven't even thought about Doug. I don't know what I'm going to do about him." She looked at Brooke, wondering if she'd see censure in her sister's eyes, but all she saw was love and concern. "I'm such a mess."

"No, you're not," Brooke said.

"Yes, I am. A pathetic mess."

Brooke rolled her eyes. "Don't forget stupid."

Kristin had to laugh. "That, too." But her smile faded quickly as she met her sister's sympathetic eyes. "Seriously, Brooke, I don't have a clue what I'm going to do about anything anymore."

Chapter Seven

Unable to face being cooped up with only his computer and the telephone for company, Nick spent most of Monday visiting old haunts. Feeling nostalgic, he drove by the theater where he used to work, but it had been torn down and replaced with a three-story office building. He wondered where the kids went to see movies nowadays. Probably in one of the cookie-cutter malls that seemed to be the new order of things everywhere.

Next he stopped by St. Lucy's, the church where he and his friends used to hang out when they were in their early teens. The church looked almost the same. The only differences seemed to be an enlarged parking lot and more mature trees on the property.

Nick had spent many an evening playing basketball in the gym and talking to Father Joe, who had been a mentor to most of the boys in the parish. They'd all looked up to the priest, who was a veteran of the Vietnam War and who seemed to understand the problems they faced. Sadly, Father Joe was no longer around to help kids. He had died of cancer five years earlier. When Nick had read about his death in the *Gazette,* it had been the one time—until now—that he'd considered returning to Green River.

Memories bombarded Nick as he walked across the parking lot to the school and entered the building housing the gym. A baby-faced priest about Nick's age was cheering on a group of youngsters playing dodgeball.

Nick watched the game for a few minutes, but when his mind started to wander to thoughts of Kristin and their last meeting, he abruptly left. He did not want to think about Kristin. He *would not* think about Kristin. His relationship with Kristin was over. It had been over for a long, long time. She was engaged to marry another man in less than two weeks. Kristin was a weakness, and Nick had no place in his life for weaknesses of any kind.

"I *will* conquer this," he muttered in what was fast becoming his battle cry.

By then it was midmorning, and he headed for the high school. He wondered if Mr. Mackintosh, his mathematics teacher and the head of the math department, was still there. He'd always liked Mr. Mackintosh, who was an excellent and creative teacher and who also had a great sense of humor and really seemed to enjoy working with adolescent kids.

Not only was the sixtyish Mr. Mackintosh still

teaching, he seemed delighted to see Nick and welcomed him warmly.

"I'm not surprised at how well you've done," the older man said, shaking Nick's hand and ushering him into his cluttered office. "I always knew you had the drive to succeed." He smiled, his gray eyes behind bifocals filled with fondness. "Not to mention the intelligence."

"Thank you. That means a lot, coming from you."

They talked for about fifteen minutes, until the bell rang for the next class. The older man gave Nick a regretful look. "I'm sorry I can't spend more time with you. But I'm teaching a class this period."

"That's all right. I understand." On impulse, he invited Mr. Mackintosh to visit him in New York. "You can spend a day with me on the floor of the exchange, see how the whole system works firsthand."

The teacher beamed. "Do you mean it?"

"Of course."

"I'd love to come."

It made Nick feel good to see his pleasure, and he was glad he'd thought to ask him. After leaving the high school, Nick finally felt ready to face his old neighborhood. It was located in an area that was literally on the other side of the tracks. In fact, one of his earliest memories was of lying in bed at night, listening to the clatter of the freight trains heading east with their loads of raw materials bound for the manufacturing plants and mills that were mostly closed today.

Grimacing, Nick slowly drove down his old street.

The neighborhood looked even worse than it had when he'd lived there. Half the buildings were boarded up and abandoned. The other half were falling down in disrepair and neglect.

He parked the Lamborghini and stared at the ramshackle frame house his family had rented for most of his boyhood. It was built in the shotgun-style, the three rooms on each of the two floors arranged in a row, one behind the other. Someone was living there, because there were clothes hung on a wash line stretched between two poles in the backyard. The laundry flapped in the October breeze.

The sight brought back so many memories, and he could almost see his mother walking out the back door and down the steps—which even then were sagging—to gather up the sheets and towels and underwear. Sometimes, if he or his brother or sister were at home, his mother would solicit their help in folding the clothes as they came off the line. In the winter, she'd hung the wash in the cellar, because the Petrillos hadn't owned a clothes dryer until Nick was in high school.

Whoever lived in the house now obviously had even less than his family had had. Everything about the place looked sad and poor. In the front yard, a faded and rusty tricycle lay on its side. Scraggly grass grew in tufts, interspersed with patches of dirt. An overflowing garbage can sat on the curb.

Nick studied the house and surrounding neighborhood for long minutes. He was glad he'd come here today. He'd *needed* to come here today. But he would never have to come again. This part of his life was over.

He started the car, turned it around and drove away.

After leaving Brooke's, Kristin spent a good part of the day with the landscaper. She tried to be enthusiastic about his plans, but it was hard to concentrate when she had so much on her mind. Somehow, though, she managed to choose what she wanted from the selections the landscaper suggested, and by the time they were finished, she was satisfied that Doug would be pleased.

After leaving the landscaper, she drove out to the mall and shopped for gifts for Brooke and Lindsay, who were going to be her only attendants at the wedding. She also purchased some toiletries for herself and a birthday present for her mother, whose birthday fell while Kristin would be on her honeymoon. Her last errand of the day was stopping at the photographer's studio where she looked at proofs of herself in her wedding finery. It took her a while, but she finally chose the shot she liked best, which would appear in the Sunday paper the morning after her wedding.

She resolutely kept her mind away from Nick.

Because she was feeling emotionally fragile and especially needy, she decided that instead of heading straight home, she would swing by Lindsay's school, which would be letting out soon, and take her to Cassidy's—one of their favorite haunts—for a hot fudge sundae. Being with Lindsay always made Kristin feel better.

Lindsay was overjoyed to see her. "Oh, good," she said, eyes lighting up. "I don't have to ride the school bus home." She happily climbed into the Mazda, and Kristin headed downtown.

She smiled as Lindsay chattered away, telling Kristin all about her day. Kristin loved listening to her. Lindsay's enthusiasm for life, her boundless energy, always gave Kristin a lift. She also liked having Lindsay to herself. Sometimes she felt guilty about this feeling—selfish, even—because she knew Meredith looked forward to seeing Lindsay at the end of the day, too.

But not today.

Maybe, after what her parents had done, Kristin would never feel guilty again.

After leaving the old neighborhood, Nick drove down Main Street on his way back to Cityside and the rental house. As he approached the town square, he saw a dark green Mazda pull into a parking slot in front of Cassidy's Ice Cream Parlor.

He slowed down.

Was that Kristin? It sure looked like her car.

Sure enough, a few seconds later, Kristin climbed out of the driver's side, and a young girl who looked to be about eleven or twelve, climbed out of the passenger side. Nick watched as Kristin slung her arm around the younger girl's shoulders and the two of them, laughing and talking, disappeared into Cassidy's. Something about the way they looked together caused a lonely ache in the vicinity of his heart.

He drove slowly past the shop. He was not paying attention to the road and had to abruptly hit the brakes when a woman pulled out of a parking place ahead. He cursed softly. Another second and he'd have put some nice dents in both his and the woman's car.

Once the woman was safely gone, Nick impulsively pulled into the vacated parking spot. Without analyzing why he was doing it, he got out of the car and, walking fast so he wouldn't change his mind, headed toward Cassidy's.

The bell tinkled, and Kristin, who was sitting facing the entrance at a table near the front of Cassidy's, looked up reflexively.

Her heart nearly stopped.

Nick!

Mind-numbing panic paralyzed her, and all she could do was stare at him as he walked over to their table. He smiled down at her and Lindsay. "Hi."

Afterward, Kristin would never know how she managed to stammer out a return greeting. "H-hi." *Omigod! What am I going to do?*

"May I join you?" His smile and the expression in his eyes was friendly and warm.

Kristin's heart was pounding in terror. She was sure he could probably hear it. Her gaze skittered to Lindsay, who was looking at her uncertainly. *Get yourself under control or she's going to know something's wrong. And so will he.* "Oh. Um…sure."

She could feel the pulse in her neck jumping. *Oh, God, please, please, please help me.*

Nick, still smiling, sat down between them. He looked at Lindsay.

Kristin swallowed. *Just calm down. Be cool. He doesn't know who she is. There's nothing to be afraid of.*

But what if he suspects?

She knew this thought was crazy. How could he possibly suspect Lindsay was his daughter? There was no way he would suspect. Why would he? Even Kristin had not suspected she was pregnant until they'd been in Europe for weeks.

Come on, calm down. The last thing you want to do is call more attention to yourself....

"This is my youngest sister, Lindsay," she said. "Lindsay, this is an old friend of mine. Nick Petrillo."

Lindsay smiled at him.

Oh, God, Kristin thought, looking from one to the other as they studied each other. She felt faint.

"Hi, Mr. Petrillo," Lindsay said.

"Please...call me Nick."

Lindsay's gaze darted to Kristin, as if to say, *Is it okay?*

Kristin wanted to cry, *No, it's not okay. None of this is okay!* and yank Lindsay up out of her chair and run as fast as her legs would carry her as far away as she could get, but she fought down the unreasonable terror and nodded her agreement.

"Nick," Lindsay said. She grinned.

While half of Kristin's mind was trying to tamp

down her panic, the other half noticed how Lindsay's irresistible smile worked its magic on Nick the same way it did on anyone who crossed her path. And his answering grin poignantly reminded Kristin of one of the reasons she'd first fallen in love with him.

"So there are now three Blair sisters," he said. "When I knew Kristin, she only had one sister—Brooke."

"I was a surprise." Lindsay's expression was impish.

Nick chuckled. "A surprise, huh?"

"Yeah, my Mom's late-in-life baby. I was born in Switzerland," she said proudly. "I have Swiss citizenship *and* American citizenship."

Oh, God, Kristin thought. *What if he puts two and two together? What if he realizes just when Lindsay was born?*

"Really?" he said. "I'm impressed."

Lindsay beamed.

"So how old are you, Lindsay?" he asked.

"Eleven. How old are *you?*"

"Lindsay!" Kristin said.

Nick couldn't help laughing at the expression on Kristin's face. Her little sister was certainly a charmer. He felt more relaxed than he'd felt in a week. "No, it's okay," he assured Kristin. "Fair is fair." He turned back to Lindsay. "I'm thirty-two. Pretty old, huh?"

He did a quick calculation. Lindsay had been born on that fateful trip to Europe, the one that had effectively removed Kristin from his life. He glanced at Kristin again, but she avoided his eyes. He suspected she was remembering, too. There was a telltale blush of pink on her cheeks.

"Thirty-two's not old," Lindsay said. "Kristin's twenty-nine and *she's* not old. And Michelle Pfeiffer's even older than that."

Nick couldn't seem to do anything but smile around this youngster, which surprised him. He didn't usually take to kids so easily. "Do you like Michelle Pfeiffer?"

"I *love* Michelle Pfeiffer. She's *so* pretty. But I think Kristin's just as pretty," Lindsay added loyally, dark eyes wide and earnest. "Don't you?"

"Lindsay!" Kristin said again, and now the blush deepened.

This time Nick didn't laugh. "Yes," he said softly, feeling a tenderness toward her that made him almost wish they were alone. Suddenly he knew exactly why he was here. He was here because he wanted to apologize to her, not only for his behavior Saturday night, but for the way he'd so coldly dismissed her yesterday. He wished he could tell her, right now, that he hadn't meant it when he'd said none of what had happened twelve years ago mattered. He'd been lying. Of course it mattered. It mattered a lot.

He also wanted to tell her he realized she was just as much an innocent bystander in this whole bloody mess as he was and that he no longer blamed her and he no longer hated her.

Instead, he continued answering Lindsay. "Just as pretty. Maybe even prettier." His gaze fastened on Kristin's mouth. Her lips were so soft. He remembered exactly how they'd felt, exactly how they'd tasted, all those times he'd kissed her. Desire, potent and powerful, flooded him. He tore his gaze from her mouth, and their eyes met. In the depths of hers, he saw awareness and something else…something that made it hard for him to breathe.

"Well, now, what can I get you folks?"

The waitress's question effectively defused the charged atmosphere. Good thing, Nick thought ruefully, because he'd been about to embarrass himself.

"What would you two ladies like?" he said, fighting to get himself and his wayward body under control. "My treat."

Kristin and Lindsay ordered hot fudge sundaes.

"That sounds good," he said. "Make it three."

"Will do," the waitress said.

While Nick talked to the waitress, Kristin struggled to get her emotions under control. Although most of her terror had abated, her emotions were still in turmoil because his behavior bewildered her. Why was he being so nice to her? And what was the meaning behind the way he'd looked at her just now? Her heart was still racing from the unexpected flash of desire she'd seen in his eyes. The *thrilling* flash of desire she'd seen in his eyes.

As casually as she could manage, she said, "So how long are you planning to be in Green River, Nick?"

He hesitated. "I'm not sure."

Something about the expression on his face told her he wasn't telling the whole truth, and once again, fear licked at her. "You must be planning to stay awhile since you've rented a house."

"The house was the only thing I could get."

"Oh?"

"Yeah, the bed-and-breakfast place was full, and I didn't like the looks of the motel."

Kristin grimaced. "I don't blame you." So maybe he wasn't planning to stay long. The thought brought mixed feelings—part relief, part something else... something Kristin didn't want to put a name to because it was suspiciously like disappointment.

"Where do you live, Nick?" Lindsay asked.

"In New York."

"Oh," she said. "I've never been to New York."

"Well, you've got lots of time. You're young."

Lindsay made a face. "I know. Mom's always telling me I'm too young for this and too young for that. I *hate* being young."

He laughed. "What about school? Do you hate school, too?"

"Oh, no, I like school."

"Good. What grade are you in?"

"Sixth."

"That means you're in, what, junior high?"

Lindsay smiled. "Uh-huh."

"I always liked school, too," he said. "What's your favorite subject?"

"Math," Lindsay said without hesitation.

"That was my favorite subject."

"It was?"

"Yes. And the work I do is a direct result of my interest in mathematics."

"Really? What do you do?"

"I manage a mutual fund."

"You mean, like on the stock exchange?"

Nick smiled. "Yes, but how do you know about the stock exchange?"

"We're studying it in school. Mrs. Evans, she's my teacher, gave each of us one thousand dollars. Well, not really...." Lindsay gave him a sheepish smile. "It's pretend, of course. Anyway, we all bought stock or mutual funds, and now we're tracking our investments."

"That's a great way to learn," Nick said. "Mrs. Evans sounds like a good teacher."

"She's the best," Lindsay said.

Kristin marveled at how easily Nick could talk to Lindsay and how comfortable she seemed to be with him. Most men weren't very interested in kids her age, and someone like Nick—high-powered and sophisticated—probably wasn't around kids much, yet he seemed perfectly at ease and he'd put Lindsay at ease.

Seeing the two of them together, listening to them talk, she couldn't help thinking what their lives might have been like if they had lived them together and raised Lindsay together. They had been cheated of so much. And Nick had been the biggest loser, because Kristin had had Lindsay all these years. He'd had nothing. The thought hurt, and suddenly she wanted to tell him how sorry she was about everything.

She wished...but what good did wishing do?

She continued to watch them.

They were so much alike.

Funny how, in the past, she'd refused to see all the things about Lindsay that were like Nick. Things that were so apparent today. Lindsay was a whiz at math, just like him. She also had his drive and intensity, his quick intelligence.

And his compassion and understanding. Those were qualities that the adult Nick had submerged—even Kristin, who hadn't seen him for so long, could see that—but he'd had them in abundance as a kid.

Kristin remembered once when she and Nick had been driving back to Green River after having spent a long Sunday afternoon picnicking in the country. They came across a young doe lying hurt at the side of the road. He immediately stopped—he'd been driving Kristin's car—and did what he could to help the wounded animal. Later, from the first pay phone they could find, he called the local animal humane society to solicit their help, then insisted on going back to where the doe lay. They waited with her until the humane society volunteer got there.

He'd always had a soft spot for the underdog, too. Another time, when he and Kristin were leaving the movie theater, they discovered three kids taunting and pushing a younger, weaker-looking boy.

Nick stopped them and gave them a good tongue-lashing. They'd skulked off, and Nick patted the younger kid on the shoulder and sent him on his way.

Lindsay was like that, too. She couldn't stand to see someone getting picked on or mistreated. In fact, she'd once punched a bully in the nose when the boy teased a classmate who stuttered.

She's the best of both of us....

The thought brought a lump to Kristin's throat as she watched father and daughter laughing and talking like old friends. She struggled against the sadness and nearly overwhelming sense of loss.

"Gee," Lindsay was saying, bringing Kristin's attention back to the conversation, "I can't wait to tell Miss Evans I met you. I'll bet *she's* never met anyone who works on the stock exchange. Will you tell me what's it like so I can tell her?"

"You ever been to the circus?"

"Yes."

"Well, that's what it's like—a three-ring circus. There's so much going on, and things are happening so fast, it's hard to keep up. People are shouting out buy and sell orders, and the board is changing all the time." He smiled. "You should get your sister to bring you to New York sometime. I'll give you both a personal tour."

Lindsay's eyes widened. "You *would?* Way *cool.* Wouldn't that be cool, Kris?"

"Yes," Kristin said faintly, "that would be cool."

Nick's gaze slowly swung her way. Her skin tingled as their eyes met again. For a moment, she could hardly breathe. She licked her lips.

Nick seemed about to say something, but before he could, their waitress returned with their order. In the flurry of serving the sundaes, the atmosphere lightened, and Kristin could breathe more easily.

"What are *you* doing now?" Nick said to Kristin.

For a moment, she was confused by the question. Then she realized he wanted to know what kind of work she did. It seemed incredible that he didn't know, and yet, how could he? "I'm a kindergarten teacher."

He considered her answer for a moment, then nodded. "Yes. I can see you doing that."

"I'm not teaching this year, though. I...I've taken a year off."

Doug had wanted her to quit teaching, period, but Kristin loved her job and didn't want to quit. She'd stood firm. It was one of the few times she'd ever opposed him, and he had been annoyed. He'd finally and reluctantly compromised. She would ask for a year's leave and, at the end of that time, if she wasn't pregnant, he guessed it would be okay if she went back to work until she *did* get pregnant. Even now, thinking about his grudging concession, Kristin felt a trickle of irritation.

"How long have you been teaching?" Nick asked.

"For six years. Ever since I graduated from college."

"Where did you end up going?"

"To the University of Hartford."

He frowned slightly, and Kristin knew he had expected her to name a school like Wellesley or Barnard—something expensive and exclusive. "How about you? Did you end up at NYU?"

"Yes."

For a long moment, he said nothing further, and Kristin wondered if he was remembering the plans they'd made, how joyfully and excitedly they'd talked about their future.

They continued to talk as they ate their sundaes,

and Kristin even managed to relax somewhat and enjoy herself. The interlude reminded her of earlier, happier times—times when she and Nick had done ordinary things together and there'd been no conflict and no tension, only happiness in each other's company.

But eventually, the sundaes were gone, and Kristin knew it was time for her and Lindsay to leave. "I'm afraid we have to go," she said.

Nick nodded, and Kristin saw the same regret she felt echoed in his eyes.

"I've enjoyed this," he said.

"Yes," Kristin said. "I have, too." She realized she meant it, despite the tension she'd felt when he had first shown up.

"It was nice meeting you, Lindsay," he said, shaking her hand as if she were a grown-up.

Lindsay beamed. "I've enjoyed meeting you, too," she said. "And thank you for telling me about the stock exchange."

"You're very welcome. I hope I'll see you again before I leave to go back home."

"Me, too."

The three of them walked out together. Nick waited as Kristin unlocked her car, then he held the passenger door open for Lindsay to get in.

Kristin started to say goodbye, but he forestalled her by saying, "Kristin, I have to see you again. Do you think we could talk?"

Kristin swallowed. "I…yes, sure."

"Tonight?"

Her mind raced. She was having dinner with Doug

at his parents' home tonight, but she knew it would be a fairly early evening. "All right, but it would have to be late."

"That's okay. What time?"

"Around eleven?"

"All right. Where?"

Kristin thought a moment. She did not want to meet him in a public place, and he certainly couldn't come to her home.

"Why don't you just come to my place?" he suggested.

She nodded her agreement.

As they drove home, Kristin was glad for Lindsay's bubbly chatter because it kept her from thinking about what she was doing.

What *was* she doing?

Why had she agreed to go to Nick's tonight? Being with him was dangerous and could only lead to trouble.

But when he'd asked her, and she'd looked into his eyes, she couldn't say no.

The trouble was, she wanted to see him again. She wanted, somehow, to resolve things between them. Maybe then, she could finally go forward.

Liar. You want to be with him. It's that simple.

"I like Nick," Lindsay said.

"Hmm?"

"I said, I like Nick."

"Yes," Kristin murmured, "I like him, too." Suddenly, she realized that, in all probability, Lindsay would tell Meredith about meeting Nick today. And then what? Her mother would be upset, and she'd probably tell her father, who would go ballistic.

For a moment, Kristin considered asking Lindsay not to say anything about Nick, because she wasn't sure she could stand another confrontation, but she quickly thought better of it. Lindsay would want to know why, and then what would Kristin say? No, it was better to just treat the encounter as the casual meeting it was.

Besides, she thought in a sudden burst of anger, she had a perfect right to talk to Nick if she wanted to. No matter what her father thought. If he got mad, that was his problem. He was the one responsible for this whole mess, anyway.

When they arrived at the house, Lindsay raced inside, heading straight for Meredith's office. Kristin followed at a more sedate pace. By the time Kristin joined her mother and Lindsay, just as Kristin had anticipated, Lindsay was already telling Meredith about meeting Nick.

"He was so nice," Lindsay said unwittingly. "I really liked him. And when I told him we were studying the stock market in school, he told me if I ever come to New York, he'll show me the stock exchange."

Meredith's eyes met Kristin's.

"Wasn't that *nice* of him?" Lindsay said. She was practically hopping up and down with excitement.

"Yes," Meredith said faintly. "Very nice." Her eyes were filled with fear.

Kristin met her mother's gaze calmly, almost defiantly. By now she'd convinced herself she had absolutely nothing to apologize for. She resolutely refused to think about what she was planning to do later that night. It was her business and hers alone.

Their gazes held for long, tense moments.

Meredith was the first to look away.

Chapter Eight

Kristin's expression shocked Meredith.

Defiant was the only way to describe it. In that moment, Meredith realized that Nick Petrillo's presence in Green River posed more of a threat to their family than she had ever imagined.

It was obvious to her that he still exerted influence over Kristin. For all Meredith knew, Kristin might still be in love with him. The ramifications, if that were true, were too horrible to comprehend.

Kristin, Doug, Edmond, Lindsay... The well-being of so many people hung in the balance.

Oh my God...

Meredith's mind whirled as fear gnawed at her. The situation was volatile and potentially disastrous. Something had to be done, but what?

Somehow she managed to keep from falling to

pieces. She even managed to answer Lindsay's comments, but she had no idea what she was saying.

Finally, Lindsay wound down and raced off to her room.

Kristin turned to go, too.

"Kristin, wait," Meredith said. She prayed for strength and wisdom. "We have to talk about this. Your father is going to be so upset when he finds out about today."

"It's not like I engineered the meeting today, Mother. It just happened."

Even though Kristin's voice was, if anything, even cooler than before, Meredith had to persevere. "But why did you stay? Why did you take such a chance? Especially when you know how your father feels?"

Kristin's mouth hardened. "What about how *I* feel, Mother?"

Before Meredith could think of a rejoinder, Kristin said, "Dad can order Lindsay around. He can even order you around. But he can't tell me who I can talk to and who I can't."

"But Kristin, why would you even want—"

"There's nothing more to say on this subject, Mother." And then, shocking Meredith even further, Kristin turned around and walked quickly out of the room.

Meredith stared after her. She couldn't believe this was happening. In the space of three days, her family's entire world was teetering on the edge of a volcano that could explode at any moment.

And Kristin!

This behavior was so unlike her. She had always

been such a wonderful daughter. Except for that one indiscretion with Nick when she was a teenager, she'd never given Meredith a moment's worry. Her temperament was sweet and caring; she rarely even raised her voice.

Brooke was the one who had inherited Edmond's temper, but Kristin...she was their sunshine girl, the peacemaker, the one who always tried to please.

But today all that had changed. There had been a determination in Kristin's eyes that Meredith had never seen before, and it filled her with a sense of dread.

She put her head in her hands, squeezing her eyes shut.

She just knew something terrible was about to happen, but just as there was no stopping that volcano once it got ready to erupt, she knew she was powerless to halt the future course of events.

Kristin dressed carefully, with much more thought than she would have if she were just going to Doug's parents for dinner. She held up several different outfits before deciding on a turquoise silk dress with a short, softly flaring skirt that enhanced and deepened the blue of her eyes and flattered her slender figure.

She also took extra care with her makeup, putting on a touch more shadow and blusher than she normally wore and dabbing perfume behind her knees and between her breasts.

She refused to think about her motives, just as she refused to feel guilty for what she planned to do.

A few minutes before seven, she descended the

stairs. She could hear her parents in the living room, having their predinner cocktail. She walked partway into the room, even though she would have preferred to avoid another encounter today.

Both parents turned. Meredith raised her glass and sipped, her eyes studying Kristin over the rim. Kristin returned her gaze steadily.

Her father smiled. "You and Doug going out?"

"Yes. We're having dinner with his parents." Her father was really something. To look at him, to hear his voice, you'd never know they'd had such a terrible argument yesterday. But he'd always had the ability to see only what he wanted to see and to wipe the rest from his mind.

"Good, good," he said. "Tell Bill and Cecily I said hello."

Meredith still said nothing.

Kristin nodded. "I will."

The doorbell rang just as the grandfather clock began to chime the hour. "That's probably Doug now. Good night, Daddy. Good night, Mother."

"Have fun," Edmond said.

"Yes," Meredith echoed. "Have fun."

Kristin thought about her parents' directive as she and Doug drove the ten miles or so to his parents' home, which was situated on a hill near the eastern outskirts of Green River. She kept stealing glances at Doug, who, as usual, was oblivious to what she was feeling.

What would Doug say, she wondered, if he had any idea what was going on in her head? If he had any inkling about the things that had happened in the past couple of days? If he had the remotest suspicion she was going to meet another man later tonight?

Would he even care?

You know darned well he'd care. You're just pretending you don't because down deep, you do feel guilty and you'd like to rationalize that guilt away.

Kristin closed her eyes.

It was going to be a long night.

After Kristin was gone, Meredith debated whether or not she should tell Edmond about today's meeting now or wait until after they'd had their dinner.

She had to tell him, even though she'd rather do anything but. If she thought Lindsay wouldn't mention meeting Nick, she wouldn't, but the chances of that happening were slim. In fact, if Meredith hadn't maneuvered Lindsay out of the house tonight, she probably would have already told him.

As it was, Meredith had only managed to postpone the inevitable by asking Brooke to invite Lindsay to dinner.

Meredith looked at Edmond, who was staring at the fireplace. He looked tired, and she'd noticed him rubbing his chest several times. She wondered if his indigestion was acting up. Sometimes, when he got upset as he had on Sunday, he would have heartburn for several days.

She decided to wait until they'd had their dinner before saying anything to him. That would give her another hour or so to formulate just the right words. Above all, she must make Edmond understand that nothing would be gained by him flying off the handle.

How she would do it, she hadn't a clue.

She only knew she must.

As the Llewellyn maid served the grilled lamb chops and fresh asparagus and tiny new potatoes she had prepared for their dinner, Kristin tried to pay attention to the conversation. Doug and his father were discussing the upcoming election, and his mother was occasionally injecting a comment. Kristin tried to make intelligent comments from time to time, too, but it was difficult because she not only found the conversation boring, she couldn't stop thinking about where she would be in just hours. With *whom* she would be.

"Are you feeling all right, darling?" Doug said, turning to her.

Kristin started. "Oh, yes, I—I'm fine."

"Are you sure? You seem a little distracted tonight."

"Oh, Doug," his mother said, laughing. "All brides-to-be are distracted this close to the wedding. You men just don't understand. Kristin has a million things on her mind." Daintily, she ate a piece of her asparagus and gave Kristin a we-women-must-indulge-these-men look.

Kristin smiled back, but inwardly she cringed. No, she didn't have a million things on her mind. Only one.

"Well, it'll all be over soon," Doug said, "and then our lives can settle down."

Settled. Kristin wasn't sure she'd ever feel settled again.

"How did your meeting with the landscaper go?" Cecily asked.

Kristin forced enthusiasm into her voice. "Very well. Thank you for recommending him. He's got great ideas."

Cecily's expression was pleased. "You know, before you leave tonight, I thought you might like to take a look at Doug's grandmother Llewellyn's cranberry glass collection. All of it will go to Doug someday, of course, but I wanted you two to have a couple of pieces to display in your new home now."

"Oh, Mrs. Llewellyn, we couldn't take your—"

"Nonsense," Cecily said. "Of course you can. I want you to. Nothing would make me happier."

The guilt Kristin had been trying so hard to suppress threatened to overwhelm her. Doug's parents were so nice. They had been lovely to her from the very beginning. Shortly after Kristin and Doug had become engaged, Cecily had told her she couldn't have handpicked a better prospective daughter-in-law than Kristin. And since then, Cecily had shown Kristin, in dozens of ways, that she'd meant every word.

Kristin swallowed, hardly able to meet Cecily's affectionate gaze. Her earlier excitement over the coming rendezvous with Nick drained away.

Why can't I love Doug the way I should?

As always, there was no answer to this question.

"What?" Edmond shouted. His face looked alarmingly red.

"Edmond, please," Meredith said. "Calm down. The only reason I told you is that I knew Lindsay would mention meeting him, and I didn't want you to think I was hiding something from you."

"How dare he follow Kristin around!"

"He wasn't following her around. It was a chance meeting."

"I don't believe in coincidence where that piece of scum is concerned. He was following her, all right." Edmond flung down his napkin. "And I'm gonna do something about it. I'm gonna fix that son of a bitch once and for all!"

And then, ignoring her pleas, he stalked from the room.

A few minutes later, Meredith heard the sound of his car careening out of the driveway.

Nick felt restless all evening. He couldn't seem to settle down to anything. He ate a light supper of a grilled-cheese sandwich and a cup of instant soup, then found a classical music station on the radio. Against the muted familiarity of a Beethoven symphony, he tried to read the new Tom Clancy novel he'd picked up in the pharmacy earlier that day.

The words kept running together. After an hour of futile effort, he finally put the book aside.

Seeing Kristin and her sister today had unearthed emotions Nick hadn't even been aware he had and made him realize, as never before, just how much he had lost twelve years ago.

He couldn't help thinking that, if things had been different, if he and Kristin had eloped the way they'd intended, they might have had a daughter like Lindsay today. Not so old, of course, but a little girl about seven or eight was a distinct possibility. Maybe they'd even have two children.

Kristin would make a wonderful mother, just as he was sure she made a wonderful teacher. She was naturally nurturing. Naturally caring.

Watching her today with her sister, he could easily imagine what she'd be like with her own child.

Nick had never given much thought to children, probably because, since Kristin, he'd given no thought to marriage. But now he realized how much he would like to have children. How much he would enjoy guiding a son or daughter, loving and caring for them the way he would have liked his father to love and care for him.

Kids were fun. They were so eager and enthusiastic, they made you see things you'd gotten too jaded to see, reexperience emotions you'd forgotten you ever had. Just the little time he'd spent talking to Lindsay today had shown him that.

He smiled. She was a great kid. How was it that Edmond Blair, who was such a complete bastard, had managed to father such terrific daughters?

He was still thinking along these lines when, a little after eight-thirty, his doorbell rang.

He frowned, glancing at his watch. It couldn't be Kristin. It was too early.

The doorbell rang again and kept ringing.

"Hold your horses," he muttered, striding to the door and yanking it open.

Before he even had a chance to react, a tight-faced Edmond Blair pushed his way past him.

Nick shut the door calmly. "Hello, *Mr.* Blair. To what do I owe this dubious honor?"

Edmond's eyes blazed. "You know damn well why I'm here, Petrillo. I told you twelve years ago to stay away from my daughter, but I guess you're the type who has to have things pounded into him."

Nick couldn't help a wry smile. Even though Edmond Blair was a fairly big man, he didn't look half as fit as Nick was, and Nick was also more than thirty years younger. "Is that a threat?" he said softly.

"Damn right, it's a threat! And you can wipe that smug smile off your face before I wipe it off for you!"

Nick was almost amused by Edmond Blair's fury. Almost, but not quite. "Your threats don't scare me. You seem to forget, your daughter is a grown woman with a mind of her own. I think she's capable of making her own decisions."

"I'm warning you!" Edmond shouted. "And you'd better listen! Because I have no intention of standing by and letting you ruin Kristin's life."

"What are you going to do? Sic the sheriff on me again? Run me out of town?"

"If I have to, yes."

Nick shrugged. "Go ahead. Give it your best shot."

Edmond glared at him. He looked ready to blow a gasket.

In contrast, Nick kept his voice even and his expression empty of emotion. "There was a time when you could hurt me. But I'm no longer powerless and scared. *You're* the one who should be scared now." He let the taunt linger in the air, savoring the look of confusion that flickered across Edmond's face and the sudden uncertainty in his eyes.

Edmond backed toward the door. "If you try to see Kristin again, I'll make you sorry you ever came back to Green River."

The threat lacked power because there was an undercurrent of fear evident in the way his voice shook, and Nick knew his subtle threat had worked. Good, he thought. Let the old bastard think about it for a while. Let him wonder. Let him squirm.

Nick strode around Edmond and opened the door. "Good night, Mr. Blair." He waited a heartbeat, then softly, aimed his parting shot. "See you at the shareholders' meeting."

Meredith worried and paced the whole time Edmond was gone. When he hadn't returned by nine-thirty, she was so afraid, she almost called the police department to ask if someone would go check the Longwell house and make sure everything was all right.

Finally, at ten o'clock, she heard his car in the driveway. "Oh, thank God," she whispered. She hurried upstairs so he wouldn't realize how concerned she'd been.

He looked shaken and ten years older when he entered their bedroom a few minutes later.

"Edmond," she said, rushing to his side. "What happened? Are you all right?"

"Yes, yes," he said, pushing her hands away. "Leave me alone." He walked to the bed and sat down heavily. His face was white and drawn, his hands shaking as he yanked at his tie.

It terrified Meredith to see him this way. "Please, Edmond," she begged. "Tell me what happened. Did...did you go to see Nick Petrillo?"

"Yes, I went to see him, all right."

"And?"

Edmond's expressionless eyes met hers. "I told him to leave Kristin alone...and he laughed at me." There was weariness and something else...fear...in his voice. "He *laughed* at me, Merry."

Meredith sat down next to him and put her arms around him. He was trembling. That frightened her more than anything. She had never seen Edmond afraid before. "Wh-what else happened?" There had to be more. Nick's laughter would have made Edmond furious, not afraid.

"He said he'd see me at the shareholders' meeting," Edmond said dully.

Meredith swallowed. She was scared to even imagine what that remark might mean.

"After I left Petrillo, I went to see Silas Guthrie," Edmond continued slowly. "He told me it's a distinct possibility that Petrillo is the one who's been buying stock in the company."

"But I thought you said there were different *companies* buying up the stock."

"Silas thinks they're dummy companies. He thinks Petrillo might be the person behind them."

"Oh, Edmond, what does that mean?"

"If it's true," he said heavily, "it can't mean anything good."

When Doug brought Kristin home just before eleven, the first floor of the house was dark except for the night-light in the kitchen. Kristin breathed a sigh of relief. It looked as if everyone was in bed, hopefully asleep.

She yawned elaborately.

"Tired?" Doug said.

"Exhausted. I had a busy day."

"Well, as I said earlier, this will all soon be over."

Kristin tried to smile convincingly. "Yes."

He put his arms around her. "Tonight was nice."

"Yes, very nice." Oh, God, she felt so guilty.

"My folks think you're wonderful."

"I like them a lot, too."

"I think we're going to have a good marriage," Doug said happily. "We think alike. We want the same things. We even have the same kind of temperament."

"Yes," she said faintly.

"I...know our relationship isn't very passionate, but you seem to feel the same way I do about that, too. That when it comes to picking a life partner, passion isn't very important."

Kristin swallowed. She had the completely irrational thought that this man was a stranger. What was she doing, marrying a stranger?

Doug tightened his arms around her. "You're cold," he murmured. "I'd better let you go in." He kissed her lightly. "Good night, darling. Get a good night's sleep, and I'll call you tomorrow."

"Good night," Kristin said weakly.

Her heart was beating too hard as she let herself in the house. She leaned against the door and closed her eyes. She felt as if she'd just run a marathon. "Nick," she whispered. "Nick."

When she finally calmed down, she continued to stand there, listening. The only sounds were normal night sounds. She hurried upstairs, not bothering to be too quiet. After all, if her parents should happen to hear her, they'd just think she was home for the night.

Once in her bedroom, she brushed her teeth and hair and dabbed on more scent. When she was ready, she tiptoed into the hall and started back down the stairs as soundlessly as she could. Just before she reached the bottom, the step squeaked. She froze. Seconds went by, and she heard nothing, so she figured it was safe to keep going.

Holding her breath, she carefully made her way to the back door, unlocked it and slipped outside.

Once she'd gained the safety of the backyard, she glanced at her parents' bedroom wing on the far side of the house. It was dark. So far, so good.

Five minutes later, she was on her way.

Meredith stood at the window. She'd parted the drapes a sliver so she could see out, but no one could see her. Behind her, Edmond snored softly.

She watched with a sinking heart as Kristin backed her car out of the garage.

* * *

When Kristin approached the Longwell house, her heart was beating harder and the excitement she'd felt earlier bubbled inside again.

The house looked welcoming. Lights were on inside and out. Kristin pulled into the driveway and drove around to the back, parking her car out of sight of the street.

Nick opened the back door as she was climbing out of the car.

Their eyes met.

Her breathing accelerated, and her heart skittered.

For a long moment, they didn't speak. The night sounds surrounded them: crickets singing, leaves rustling in the night breeze, a dog barking somewhere nearby.

And then, whispering, "Kristin," he opened his arms, and she walked into them.

Chapter Nine

The moment Kristin felt the touch of Nick's lips against hers, the last twelve years disappeared as if they had never existed. All of the emotions, all of the desires, all of the needs buried for so long, erupted into life.

She melted against him and let the world spin around her. She felt boneless, all liquid heat, as lips met lips, tongue met tongue, body met body.

And heart met heart.

The rightness of it stunned her, and Kristin knew then that she loved him. She had always loved him. She *would* always love him.

No one else existed for her...or ever would.

They kissed again and again there in the moonlight, sheltered from prying eyes by the house and the trees and the shadowed night.

They needed no words. Their straining hearts and eager hands and lips said everything that needed saying. They wanted each other. They needed each other. And soon, very soon, they would go inside and make love to each other.

On some level, Kristin knew she shouldn't make love with Nick. Not tonight. Not until she'd broken off her engagement to Doug. But she couldn't seem to help herself. Her need was too great. She had been deprived for too long.

When the kisses were no longer enough, when each wanted and needed more, when only a complete union would satisfy them, Nick took her hand and led her into the house. They went straight into his bedroom.

Kristin felt as if she were moving in a dream. Nothing seemed real. And yet everything had more clarity. Afterward, she never remembered undressing. One moment the two of them were standing in Nick's bedroom fully clothed, the next their clothes were in a tangled pile on the floor and they were lying in bed, arms and legs entwined.

"Nick, oh Nick," Kristin murmured as his hands and lips molded and caressed. She closed her eyes and savored the wonder, the sheer ecstasy of loving him and wanting him. Of him loving her and wanting her.

Oh, she'd missed this.

Oh, she needed this.

She gave herself up to the feelings and just let herself float in sensation and warmth and happiness. Now that they knew what would happen between them tonight, their kisses were slower, sweeter, softer.

"Kristin," he whispered. His hands trembled as he stroked her. He was deeply moved by her trust, by the way she had simply walked into his arms tonight, by her willingness and passionate response to him. It was as if the intervening years, the ones where they'd been apart, had never been. She was as familiar to him as he was to himself—a part of him. How could he have forgotten?

She gave so much. He marveled at her giving. She was the most generous person he'd ever known. The sweetest, the most loving. He wished he had the words to tell her how he felt, how special she was, and how much he'd missed her and wanted her all these years—even when he hadn't been willing to admit the missing and wanting. But words had never come easy for him, especially words of love. The most deeply felt emotions had always been the hardest to express, so he contented himself now with showing her how much she meant to him.

He touched her almost reverently, worshiping her body with his eyes and hands and mouth. Each time she moaned softly or whispered his name, it thrilled him and made him want to give her even more pleasure.

He could have looked at her forever. She was so beautiful. Her skin felt so warm and soft. She smelled so good. She tasted so good. He loved touching her. Loved the quick intake of breath, the involuntary little moan, when he found a particularly sensitive place.

And when she touched him!

He had to close his eyes and grit his teeth and force himself not to crush her to him and take her too fast. But finally, he could wait no longer. He was too aroused. He needed her too much.

He raised himself over her and looked down into her eyes. And then she was urging him inside her and he was encircled by heat and warmth. They moved together, slowly at first, then faster as they found their rhythm.

There was nothing in the world like this. Nothing that compared to the exquisite torture that built into a shattering crescendo of sensation that made you feel as if you were falling apart.

Nick held her tightly and wished he never had to let her go.

Afterward, as their bodies cooled and their breathing slowed, Kristin lay in the circle of Nick's arms and waited for him to say he loved her and wanted to marry her.

But he said nothing.

Instead, he smoothed her hair back from her face, kissed her forehead and held her close.

She wasn't worried, she decided. He just needed time. He had given her his heart once and look what had happened. He would be very careful and very sure before he exposed himself to that kind of hurt again.

He loved her. She knew he did. His actions tonight had shown her the way he felt. And in time he would tell her. She could wait.

But, in the meantime, she would have to tell Doug she couldn't marry him. In fact, she would have to tell him immediately. Tomorrow. It was the only right thing to do. She shivered a little, thinking about it.

"You're not sorry, are you?"

Nick must have felt her involuntary shudder. She snuggled closer. "No, I'm not sorry."

He stroked her arm, let his hand trail down to the swell of her hip. "I thought I'd forgotten you, but I never did."

"I know," she whispered.

He was silent for a long time. "Kristin? Did you think about me...at all...during the past twelve years?"

Did she think about him? Kristin remembered about all the nights she'd cried herself to sleep with a pillow over her head so her parents and Brooke wouldn't hear her. She remembered the night Lindsay was born, in the middle of a snowstorm, in a private, very secluded Swiss hospital where money could buy anything, even a birth certificate with whatever information you wanted it to contain.

She remembered how, afterward, she had held her tiny daughter in her arms and how the tears had run down her cheeks and how much she had wished Nick were there with her. How on every one of Lindsay's birthdays she had wondered where he was and what he was doing and if he ever thought of her. How on Christmas mornings and Easter mornings and the anniversary of the day they'd met she'd thought of him and how much he was missing. How every time she went to Primrose Hill she saw their initials in the copper beech tree and she would remember things he'd said and done.

Did she think of him?

When *hadn't* she been thinking of him?

She sighed deeply, moving slightly so she could kiss the hollow of his neck. "I thought about you far too much for my own good. How about you? Did you think of me?"

"I told myself I wasn't, but down deep, you were always there." He chuckled. "You spoiled every other woman for me."

She laughed softly. "Next you'll be telling me you were true to me all this time," she teased.

His answer was slow in coming. "In my heart I was."

The words brought a lump to her throat, because she could hear the honesty in his voice and she knew what he said was true.

He did love her.

And soon he would tell her so.

Nick watched Kristin sleep. He didn't want to disturb her, because she looked so peaceful and contented, but he knew she couldn't stay all night. If anyone saw her car, it would cause a scandal. For himself, he didn't care what anyone thought or said, but he did care for Kristin's sake. Plus he didn't want to cause her unnecessary problems with her family.

There would be enough trouble in that area later, he thought ruefully. He wondered what Kristin would think when she found out about her father's visit to him this evening. Nick had considered telling her right after they'd first made love, but she seemed so happy, and he was feeling so happy himself, he hated to introduce such a discordant element. Now he wondered if he should tell her when she woke up. For some reason, he still felt reluctant to say anything. Maybe he'd just wait and see how things went between them first.

That settled, he looked at the bedside clock, saw that it was two o'clock, and reluctantly decided it was time to wake her.

So he leaned over and kissed her cheek, then her neck, then her shoulder. He slipped his hand under the covers and gently cupped her breast.

She sighed and stirred, still half-asleep, and turned toward him. She snuggled into his arms.

He couldn't help himself.

He wanted to make love to her again. He tipped her chin up and kissed her on the mouth, parting her lips with his tongue and kissing her deeply. Within moments, she responded by kissing him back, and soon they were lost to everything but each other.

At three o'clock, Kristin reluctantly got up and got dressed. Nick lay in bed and watched her.

"Slug," she teased. "I hate you because you can stay there and I have go out in the cold."

He laughed. "Don't forget the part about having to walk two miles in the snow."

She picked up her shoe and threw it at him. He ducked and it hit the headboard.

"Watch it, woman," he said. "Or I might have to get up and teach you a lesson."

"Oh, really?"

"Really."

Kristin was about to tell him to give it his best shot, but she knew she couldn't stay any longer. She had to get home. So she just shook her head and muttered, "Men," and zipped up her dress.

When she was ready to leave, he slid out of bed and pulled on his briefs, then his pants. In the few seconds while he was still naked, Kristin admired the way he looked. His body was sleek and hard and nicely muscled, and she knew he must work out often. Of course he would. Nick would approach taking care of his body the way he approached everything else: with single-minded doggedness and determination.

"Like what you see?" he said, smiling.

"Very much."

Their eyes met for a moment. "I'll walk you out," he said softly.

"All right."

When they reached her car, he held her close for a long moment. Then he kissed her once, hard, and said, "Now we really need to talk. I'll call you tomorrow."

"No," she said quickly. "Better not. I'll call you." She wanted to add that she loved him, but she didn't want to pressure him into thinking he had to say the words until he was ready, so she contented herself with saying, "Tonight meant a lot to me."

"Yes," he said. "To me, too."

"Good night."

"Good night."

She drove home in a giddy daze. She couldn't remember when she'd felt so wonderful. So happy. And so completely sure that everything in her life was finally on the right track.

Still, underlying the happiness was the knowledge that sometime in the next twenty-four hours she would have to tell Doug and her parents that the wedding was off. Ironically, telling Doug would probably be easiest, because she didn't think he would care all that much—except maybe for his pride that would be hurt.

But her parents!

They would be incredibly upset. Her father would have a fit. Well, he'd just have to have the fit and get over it. Because no matter how angry he was or what he said or did or threatened to do, Kristin wasn't going to change her mind. She loved Nick and only Nick. She had lost him once. She did not intend to lose him again.

She smiled. Tonight had been so incredible. She had forgotten how wonderful it was to be with a man you adored and wanted passionately. But that wasn't entirely true. She hadn't really forgotten. She had just submerged the knowledge, because to allow it to come to the surface would have meant having to face truths she didn't want to face.

Lost in thought, she rounded the corner of Acorn Street, where her parents' home stood at the end of the block.

Suddenly her eyes widened in shock. The house

was ablaze with light, and there was an ambulance, red lights flashing, sitting in the driveway.

Oh, God!

Something had happened.

Heart pumping like a piston, Kristin screeched to a stop in front of the house, yanked the door open and raced up the lawn. The front door stood wide open, and as Kristin, horrified, watched, two EMS attendants carrying a stretcher, walked out the door toward the open ambulance. Kristin's mother was behind them.

"Mother!" Kristin shouted. "What's wrong? What's happened?"

Her mother's expression was accusatory as her gaze swung briefly to Kristin. "Your father has had a heart attack." Her voice didn't sound like her at all.

"Oh, no...." Kristin's hand covered her mouth. Her mother's expression told her that Meredith suspected where she'd been tonight. Guilt flooded her. "I—is he going to be all right?"

"I hope so," Meredith said, and it was obvious she was trying not to lose control. "I'm going to the hospital in the ambulance."

"I'll follow in the car."

"Kris." Lindsay ran down the steps, her face white and frightened, tears glistening in her eyes. "Don't leave me! I want to go, too."

"Oh, honey, I wouldn't leave you."

Milly, wrapped in a terry-cloth robe, face set in sober lines, walked out onto the stoop. "You'll call me when you know anything, won't you?" she said.

"Of course," Kristin said. "C'mon, Lindsay, let's go."

As the ambulance careened out of the driveway and drove off, siren wailing, Kristin and Lindsay walked across the lawn to Kristin's car.

The county hospital was a twenty-minute drive away, and by the time they arrived, Edmond had been admitted and was already in the cardiac-care unit. Kristin and Lindsay hurried upstairs and found their mother in the waiting room outside swinging double doors.

"Mom, I'm sorry," Kristin said, walking over to her mother and taking her in her arms.

Meredith's body trembled. "I'm so scared," she whispered.

"I know."

"Th-they wouldn't let me go in there. I—I had to wait out here."

"I know," Kristin said again. "C'mon, let's go sit down." She put her arm around her mother's shoulders, and with her other hand, reached for Lindsay. The three of them sat huddled together on the leather couch facing the doors.

Tears were running down Meredith's cheeks. It shocked Kristin to see how fragile and...old...her mother looked. Meredith had always been such a rock that this display of vulnerability was all the more disconcerting. She took her mother's hand, and Meredith gripped Kristin's tightly.

"What happened?" Kristin asked.

Meredith closed her eyes. "It was awful," she murmured. "Awful." She drew a long, shaky breath, then opened her eyes and looked at Kristin. "He...he was upset earlier...." Her gaze moved beyond Kristin, to Lindsay. "Lindsay, sweetheart, would you mind going back to the nurses' station? There's a room there with a Coke machine. Maybe you could get us all something to drink."

"Okay."

Once Lindsay was safely out of earshot, Meredith told Kristin everything that had happened. How she'd told Edmond about Kristin and Lindsay meeting Nick at the ice-cream parlor earlier in the day because she knew Lindsay would mention his name and felt she'd better tell Edmond first.

"Yes," Kristin said. "You were right to do that."

"But, oh, Kristin, he got so angry. He charged out of the house and went over to the Longwell house, and he and Nick had it out."

He and Nick had it out?

As the significance of her mother's words sank in, a heavy feeling of dread filled her. Why hadn't Nick told her? While Meredith repeated the conversation between her father and Nick, Kristin listened in shocked silence.

Had tonight been a lie?

Hadn't it meant *anything* to him?

She remembered how he hadn't said he loved her. Did he make love to her tonight just to prove he could?

She hated feeling this way, but how could she feel any other way? Obviously, Nick had not told her about the confrontation with her father because he had some ulterior reason for keeping it hidden.

And what other reason could there be, except that he was afraid if she'd known about her father's visit and what they'd said to one another, she wouldn't have stayed.

"After he came home, he told me that Silas Guthrie thinks Nick is the person behind this big buyout of the company stock," Meredith continued.

"That couldn't be true," Kristin said. But she was afraid. Very afraid. What if it were true? What would that mean?

"Your father was so worried. He looked exhausted, and he went right to bed. Then, about fifteen minutes before you came home, I heard him get up. He only walked a few feet when he collapsed. Thank God I took that CPR course, so I knew exactly what to do. I shouted for Lindsay to call 911, and then I did rescue breathing and chest compressions until the EMS showed up."

"Oh, Mom, God, I'm sorry. I should have been there with you."

Her mother's eyes met hers again. "You were with *him,* weren't you?"

There had been too many lies. It was time for the truth. "Yes."

"Oh, Kristin, how *could* you? How could you do that to Doug?"

Kristin swallowed. "I know I should have waited, but I plan to tell Doug today that I can't marry him."

Meredith gripped Kristin's shoulder. "Please don't do that. Please. Your father... I don't know if he can take that kind of news. Please, darling, please wait."

Just then Lindsay returned with three cans of cold

drinks, so Kristin could only say, "Okay, Mother, don't worry. I promise. I won't do anything until we know how Dad is."

Chapter Ten

It was a hellish night.

Kristin, Meredith and Lindsay waited and waited and waited. From time to time, Lindsay dozed off, sleeping with her head against Kristin's shoulder, but for the most part, the three of them were awake and worried.

Several times, Meredith's bottom lip trembled, and Kristin put her arms around her mother and murmured encouragement, saying things like, "Don't worry, Mom. He's in good hands. I'm sure everything will be all right." Kristin only hoped what she was saying was true.

During these long hours, Kristin had plenty of time to think. Too much time, especially when her thoughts were filled with so much turmoil. Over and over again, she thought about what had happened between her and Nick earlier, and all the things he hadn't said.

She also thought about her father.

Her father was far from perfect. She knew that. And he had done some terrible things to her, things that, until this moment, she hadn't been sure she could ever fully forgive.

But he was still her father, and she loved him. And even though wrong, he had believed he was acting in her best interest. She didn't want to punish him, and she certainly didn't want to hurt him or upset him any more than he'd already been.

But she was going to hurt him when she broke off her engagement to Doug. And she *was* going to break it off. That hadn't changed, no matter what else had.

More than once, she'd walked to the window and stared out at the sleeping city beyond. How had things gotten to be in such a mess? Her troubled thoughts, in addition to her lack of sleep, gave her a vicious headache. She sighed wearily, wondering if the night would ever be over.

Finally, just when Kristin was beginning to think something must be terribly wrong and the medical staff was avoiding the family because they didn't want to tell them bad news, Dr. Palmer, the cardiac specialist and a family friend, came out to the waiting area to talk to them.

Lindsay, big-eyed, slipped her hand into Kristin's, and Kristin squeezed comfortingly, although her heart stuttered in fear. Dr. Palmer looked so tired. His expression was so serious.

Kristin held her breath, afraid to look at her mother. *Please, God, please let Daddy be okay.*

"Simon," Meredith said, jumping up and rushing forward as soon as she saw him. "How is he? Is he okay? Can I see him?"

"Now, Meredith, calm down," Dr. Palmer said. He led her back to the couch, made her sit, then pulled a chair over so he could sit facing her. "For now he's out of the woods."

"Oh, thank God," Meredith said, shoulders sagging in relief.

Kristin silently echoed her mother's thanks. Weak with relief, she smiled down at Lindsay, who gave her a tremulous smile back.

"But I'm not going to kid you," Dr. Palmer continued gravely, his gaze sweeping to include Kristin and Lindsay, too. "This was a major heart attack, and his heart has sustained a lot of damage. The only reason he pulled through at all is because you—" he reached over and patted Meredith's hand "—kept such a level head and were able to administer CPR and keep him alive until the emergency medical crew got there." His smile was kind. "You did good, my dear."

A tear rolled down Meredith's cheek. She brushed it aside. "H-he's stabilized now, isn't he, Simon?"

"Yes. He seems to be."

"So he should be all right."

"I think so," Dr. Palmer said. "I hope so. We'll be able to tell better tomorrow. The first twenty-four hours after an attack are crucial. If he weathers them without another attack, he should begin to recover."

Meredith closed her eyes. Her throat worked. Kristin put her arm around her mother's shoulders and felt the tremor snaking through her. "So...what do we do?" she finally said. She took a deep, shaky breath.

"All we can do is watch him closely, wait...and pray. Then, if all goes well, Edmond will be released to go home. But I have to warn you, Meredith, even then, it will be imperative that you and the rest of the family keep his life peaceful and calm and as free of stress as you can manage. Because the next attack could be fatal."

Kristin's attention wandered as he continued to talk to her mother, describing medically exactly what had happened to Kristin's father and what they could expect in the days and weeks ahead. She knew she should listen carefully, but the doctor's warning kept going round and round in her head.

It will be imperative that you...keep his life peaceful and calm and as free of stress....

What was this directive going to mean in terms of her plan to break her engagement to Doug? If she went ahead with it and they called off the wedding, there would be no way to keep the news from her father. He would find out, and he would be so upset, it could trigger another attack.

Dear heaven.

How could she take that chance?

She couldn't.

She simply couldn't. She would have to wait, at least for the twenty-four-hour period Dr. Palmer had mentioned as being the crucial time.

But maybe not. Maybe she could still tell Doug how she felt, but ask him if he'd be willing to pretend everything was all right between them until her father was out of the woods and could take the news of their breakup better.

But was that fair to Doug? And even if he agreed, how could they pull it off when the wedding was less than two weeks away? Wouldn't her father know something was wrong if things didn't go ahead on schedule?

Kristin bit her lip in consternation.

Maybe they could say they were postponing the wedding indefinitely because they wanted to wait until Edmond was completely well and could participate.

Breaking into her thoughts and reclaiming her attention, Dr. Palmer rose and said, "You can go in and see him now."

Kristin struggled to banish the dilemma of her engagement. "All of us?" she asked.

"No. It's best if it's just your mother right now," he said. "You ready, Meredith?"

"Yes."

"Now remember, he looks bad, so I want you to be strong. It won't do him any good to have you break down."

"I won't."

"Good. Let's go, then."

Meredith turned to Kristin. "While I go see your father, will you call Doug? Tell him to let all of them at work know what's happened?"

"Of course." Kristin looked at her watch. It was

a little after seven. She could probably catch Doug at home. "What about Brooke? Do you want me to call her now, too?"

Meredith sighed. "I guess we can't put it off much longer. You know how fast news travels in Green River, and I sure wouldn't want her finding out from someone other than us." Her face twisted into new lines of concern. "Oh, dear, I hate to upset her in her condition."

"Don't worry, Mom," Kristin said. "I'll break it to her gently. In fact, if I call her first, I should get Chandler at home, too. He can calm her down if she gets too upset."

After giving her blessing to Kristin's plan, Meredith, along with Dr. Palmer, disappeared through the double doors into the cardiac-care unit.

Kristin turned to Lindsay. "C'mon, honey, let's go find a pay phone." They found one around the corner, and while Lindsay waited quietly a few feet away, Kristin dialed Brooke's home first, praying Chandler would answer the phone.

She was in luck. His cheerful voice said a bright hello.

"Hi, Chandler, it's Kristin."

"Well, hello, sister-in-law. You're up bright and early."

"Yes, well..." She quickly told him what had happened and what the doctor had said. "Do you want to tell Brooke, or should I?"

"I think it's better if I do," he said carefully. He lowered his voice, and Kristin figured Brooke was nearby. "What's the number there? I'm sure she'll want to call you back."

Kristin gave it to him, then quickly dialed Doug's number. He answered on the second ring.

"Kristin, I'm so sorry," he said after she'd explained. "And yes, of course, I'll call Silas and the others to let them know. Ginny, too." Ginny was Edmond's secretary of twenty-some years. "Do you want me to come sit with you?"

"Oh, Doug, I appreciate the offer, but I think you'll do more good if you go into the office and take care of things in Daddy's absence." Kristin knew she was being a coward, but she wasn't sure she could face Doug right now.

"I think you're right," he agreed. "But I'll come tonight."

"Good."

"And Kristin?"

"Yes."

"Tell your mother not to worry. I'll take care of everything. After all, this is what your father's been grooming me for. It's just going to happen a little sooner than we expected."

Kristin could have sworn there was an edge of unseemly excitement in his voice. Oh, she was probably just imagining it, she told herself as she hung up. Surely Doug wouldn't be *excited* about her father's heart attack, would he? She was getting punchy from lack of sleep.

Next, Kristin called Milly because she knew the housekeeper would be worried, and when Milly asked what she could do to help, Kristin suggested she drive over to the hospital and pick up Lindsay.

"But I want to stay here," Lindsay protested.

"Honey, there's absolutely nothing you can do here, and they won't even let you see Daddy until tonight probably. No, I think it's better that you go home and get some sleep. Later this afternoon, if Daddy's up to seeing us, Milly can bring you back to the hospital."

"Well, okay..." Lindsay said reluctantly.

A few minutes later, Brooke called.

"Oh, God, Kris, this is *awful,*" she said when Kristin answered.

The sisters talked a few minutes, then Brooke said she would get ready and drive over to the hospital.

"Okay, see you in a little while," Kristin said.

Now that all the necessary calls were taken care of, Kristin and Lindsay walked back to the waiting area. About ten minutes later, Meredith rejoined them.

She seemed relieved and more optimistic, saying, "He was too foggy with medicine to talk, and he kept falling asleep, but he knew me. He smiled at me."

Kristin told her mother about her phone conversations with Doug and Milly and Brooke. "After Milly comes for Lindsay, maybe you and I can go get some coffee and something to eat," she suggested.

"I'm not hungry."

"Mom, you'll feel better if you eat something. You've got to keep up your strength."

Meredith sighed. "Oh, all right."

Milly got there in record time. Once she and Lindsay were gone, Kristin and Meredith headed for the cafeteria. Kristin wouldn't let her mother go back to the cardiac-care unit until she'd watched her eat all of a bran muffin and most of a dish of grapefruit sections. Then, carrying cups of coffee with them, they returned to the floor.

Silas Guthrie was there waiting for them. He took Meredith's hands, saying, "I'm so sorry, Meredith, but I knew something like this would happen someday. Edmond gets too upset about things."

Kristin bit back a smile. If that wasn't the pot calling the kettle black. Silas was one of the most intense worrywarts she'd ever met. Her mother laughed about Silas all the time, calling him an old lady and a fussbudget.

"Is it what I told him about the stock that caused this to happen, do you think?" Silas asked, his brow creasing.

Meredith shook her head. "No. And I don't want you blaming yourself, Silas. Something else happened yesterday to upset him. He had a terrible argument with Nick Petrillo and Nick said something to him that frightened him." She quickly explained.

"Well, he was right to be frightened," Silas said darkly. "Because I did some checking and found out our worst fears are true. Petrillo is definitely the person behind the stock buyout."

Kristin felt as if Silas had hit her. In fact, if he had hit her, she couldn't have been more shocked. What in the world was all this about? And why was this the first time she'd heard of it? She wanted to question her mother then and there, but she held her tongue until Silas left.

Then she immediately demanded that her mother tell her everything. Afterward, Kristin sat there stunned, trying to take it all in.

Nick had bought up huge amounts of Blair Manufacturing stock, in the names of various companies he controlled, over the past three or four years. Why?

There was only one explanation. He was planning to do something to hurt her father through the company. That had to be it. What other reason could there be?

And he must *still* be planning something, because if he wasn't, he would have told her about her father's visit. He would have told her about buying the stock. And after he'd explained, he would have said something like, "But now, of course, everything's changed."

But he hadn't said a single word.

And that could only mean he hadn't changed his mind about anything.

Which meant he didn't love her. Which meant she'd been deluding herself. Which meant he had only made love to her to get even, just as he somehow planned to get even with her father.

Nick didn't sleep after Kristin left. He couldn't. His emotions were too raw, and he had too much to think about. About six o'clock, he finally got up and made a pot of coffee. While it was brewing, he dressed in sweats and running shoes. He drank his first cup standing up, then headed out into the crisp, just-beginning-to-get-light autumn morning and ran for forty-five minutes.

He'd always found workout time to be good thinking time, and today was no exception. By the time he returned to the house, he knew three things: he loved Kristin and wanted her back in his life, he despised Edmond Blair more than ever and he and Kristin needed to get things settled between them. Nick felt sure, after last night, that Kristin loved him, too. Now he needed to know what she planned to do about her engagement to Doug Llewellyn.

He stripped off his sweaty clothes, showered, drank more coffee and fixed a light breakfast. While eating, he read the morning paper, which he'd arranged to have delivered while he was in Green River. Then, deciding it was too early for Kristin to call him, he figured he was safe and wouldn't miss her call if he went out to buy the *Wall Street Journal*.

By lunchtime, he'd read the paper from cover to cover, called his office and taken care of a few problems, sent half a dozen faxes and talked to several nervous Nellie clients. He'd also looked at his watch a dozen times. He was sure she'd call first thing this morning.

By one o'clock, when Kristin still hadn't called, impatient and growing worried, he considered calling her house. After all, the housekeeper would probably answer the phone, and she wouldn't know Nick's voice. Why not? He wouldn't leave a message, so there'd be no harm done if Kristin wasn't there. And if the housekeeper wanted to know his name before calling Kristin to the phone, he would simply say he was a friend of a friend.

He picked up the phone.

But the housekeeper did not ask his name.

She said, "I'm sorry, sir, Miss Kristin isn't here. She and her mother are at the county hospital, because Mr. Edmond, he had a heart attack in the middle of the night and that's where they took him."

Nick thanked her and quietly hung up. He stood tapping his pen against the table and staring off into space for a long time. So Edmond Blair had had a heart attack in the middle of the night. How severe an attack? he wondered. And had it happened before or after Kristin arrived home? The news was sobering, coming as it had right after his confrontation with Edmond yesterday evening. Could that argument, culminating as it had with Nick's warning, have had anything to do with Edmond Blair's attack?

Nick swallowed. He hated Edmond Blair, yes, and he wanted to see him suffer, yes, but he'd wanted the suffering to be *mental*, not physical. He'd wanted Edmond to agonize over events, to wallow in regret for a long, long time. Nick had *never* wished something like this to happen.

Damn! He hoped their argument wasn't the cause of the attack. Guilt swept him as he remembered how upset and frightened Edmond had been and how he, Nick, had threatened the older man.

But Nick pushed the guilt away.

Why should *he* feel guilty?

He had done nothing wrong.

Edmond Blair was the one who should be feeling

guilty. He was the one who had charged over to the house last night and told Nick to get out of town. He was the one who thought he was God and was trying to control everyone's life.

If he'd stayed out of Nick's and Kristin's business in the first place, none of this would have happened.

Kristin stayed at the hospital all day. She and Brooke and Meredith took turns going in to see Edmond. Kristin hated the sight of her father hooked up to so many machines. He looked so old and sick and helpless. Tears sprang into her eyes as she watched him doze. Her heart was heavy with remorse and the wish that, somehow, she could have done something to avert this. And then she would tell herself that the heart attack was not her fault, but the guilt refused to go away.

About two o'clock, Kristin called the house and told Milly not to bring Lindsay to the hospital that afternoon. "She'll be upset, because I told her she could come, but there's just no reason for her to be here. Tell her I'll call her later."

"You're right, Miss Kristin," Milly said. "I'll distract her by getting her to help me bake Mr. Edmond's favorite peanut butter cookies. I'll tell her when her dad is well enough, she can take him some."

"You're a genius, Milly."

Doug and Chandler both showed up shortly after five. Once again, Kristin had the unsettling feeling that Doug was secretly thrilled to have this chance to run the company.

"Tell Edmond he doesn't have to worry," he kept saying to Meredith. "I'm happy to take care of everything at the office."

Kristin knew it was wrong of her to question Doug's motives. After all, one of the reasons her father was so thrilled about her engagement to Doug was that Doug was slated to take over when Edmond retired. Doug would be the son Edmond had not had. So what did it matter if Doug was eagerly assuming the reins of the company now? Better that he should be eager instead of reluctant, confident instead afraid. At least her father would not have to worry about the company falling apart in his absence.

After Chandler and Brooke left to go home—with Brooke protesting she was fine and Chandler insisting she needed to get some rest—Doug offered to stay if they wanted him to.

Both Kristin and Meredith told him to go home; there was nothing he could do that he wasn't already doing.

About eight o'clock, Dr. Palmer arrived. He went in to check on Edmond, then came back out to talk to them. He said Edmond was resting quietly, that everything looked good, and suggested that the two of them go home and get some sleep. "You can't do anything here," he said, echoing the same thing Kristin had said to Milly and she and her mother had said to Doug. "You don't have to worry. The night supervisor knows to call you if there's any change. Come back in the morning, and we should have a pretty good idea of his prognosis by then."

Kristin's mother made a halfhearted protest, but

both the doctor and Kristin overruled her. Meredith gave in without further argument, and Kristin knew this had to mean Meredith was completely worn-out. Otherwise, wild horses wouldn't have dragged her from her vigil.

When they arrived at the house, Meredith confirmed Kristin's feelings. "I think I'll take a hot bath and go to bed," she said, her face pale and drawn.

"Good," Kristin said. She was exhausted, too, but she couldn't let herself give in to the exhaustion. She had more pressing business. She had to talk to Nick. So after her mother was settled, she spent an hour or so reassuring Lindsay that all would be well again, then headed to her own room.

She showered and changed into jeans and a red cable-knit sweater. Pulling her hair back into a ponytail, she secured it with a red ribbon. She eyed the phone, wondering if she should call Nick first. She decided not to. She would just take her chances.

Then she walked downstairs and told Milly she had to go out for a while. Milly didn't question her, and Kristin was glad. She wasn't in the mood to answer any questions.

Nick was home. The garage was open, and she could see his car.

Not caring anymore who might see her car, Kristin parked on the street. She was perfectly calm, perfectly composed as she walked to the door and rang the bell. She'd done so much thinking and worrying throughout the long day, she had reached a kind of fatalistic attitude.

She wasn't angry.

She had not jumped to conclusions.

Yes, the evidence against Nick looked damning, but she would ask him about his motives for buying the stock and give him a chance to explain. And then, whatever happened, happened. She had survived some tough situations in her life. If she had to, she could survive another.

When Nick opened the door, he was not surprised to see Kristin standing there. As always, she looked beautiful to him, even though her face was pale and there were circles of fatigue under her eyes.

"Hi," he said, reaching for her hand and drawing her inside. "I was hoping it was you. I heard what happened." He gave her a sympathetic smile.

"Did you? Who told you?"

"Your housekeeper. When I didn't hear from you, I called the house."

She nodded. He wanted to draw her into his arms. Comfort her. Tell her he knew what a bad day she'd had. But there was an aloofness and distance about her that held him back. Unsmiling, she walked past him, into the living room, then turned to face him. "Is it true?" she said without preamble.

Nick's heart gave a guilty jump. "Is what true?"

"Don't play games with me, Nick. You know what I mean. Is it true that you've been buying stock in my father's company for years now?"

Nick considered hedging. He did not want to expose his hand before the board meeting. And if anyone but Kristin were asking the question, he *would*

hedge. But it *was* Kristin. And there had been enough
lies. "Yes," he said quietly. "I have."

"Why, Nick?"

He shrugged. "It's what I do."

"Are you saying you bought the stock with your
fund's money? That it's part of the portfolio you've
put together for your investors?"

He shook his head. "No."

"So the stock you've bought, you've bought for
yourself."

Nick met her gaze squarely. "Yes."

She closed her eyes briefly, then sighing, she said,
"You're planning something, aren't you? You
bought all this stock for a reason. Somehow you plan
to ruin my father, don't you?"

"If by 'ruin,' you mean take over the company,
then, yes, that's what I plan."

She stared at him, her eyes dark and unhappy.
"Still? You're *still* planning to hurt my father? Did
what happened between us last night mean *nothing*
to you?"

Suddenly, the guilt he'd felt off and on all day
vanished completely in the wake of the incredulity
he'd heard in her voice, an incredulity he couldn't
understand. Surely, she, of all people, knew he had
a perfect right to hate her father. "I don't see how
what happened last night changes anything," he
countered. "If the shoe were on the other foot, your
father wouldn't think a thing of grinding me into the
ground."

"But the shoe isn't on the other foot." When he
didn't answer, her gaze clung to his for long, quiet

seconds. Finally she spoke. "If you really cared about me, Nick, you wouldn't do this."

Nick knew, on some level, that what she'd just said was true, but emotionally, all he could hear was that she was more concerned about her father and the company than she was about him. "If you really cared about *me*," he responded tightly, "you'd say to hell with everyone else. I love you, Kristin. I want you to go away with me. I want you to tell me, now, that nothing else matters except us."

He could see she was struggling for control. Her eyes glistened with tears. "You want me to turn my back on my family? Leave Green River and never look back? Never see my parents...my sisters...again? Is that what you're saying?"

He wanted so much to take her into his arms and tell her everything would be okay, that they could work this out, but he hardened his heart. "I'm saying it's time for you to choose between your father and me."

"No," she whispered sadly, shaking her head. "No. The time has come for *you* to choose, Nick. The past. Or the future. Anger and revenge or love and hope." She waited, her eyes imploring him. Then, when he stood stonily, her shoulder slumped in weariness. "You know, up until this moment, I thought I loved you, too. But now I see everything so clearly. And I realize that I love the man you were, not the man you've become. I could never hurt my family the way you want me to. Two wrongs never make a right. What my father did years ago, it was awful, and it hurt us, I know that. I'm not excusing him. But he acted out of love for me. He really thought he was doing the right thing.''

Nick smiled cynically even though her words had been like stones pounding his heart. ''I see. It's okay to do any despicable thing as long as you believe you're right. Well, I believe I'm right about this.''

Now her tears were falling freely. But her voice was steady. ''I know you won't believe this, Nick, but we could never have built any kind of happiness on the ashes of my family.'' She walked closer, raising her right hand to touch his cheek. Then she reached up on tiptoe and kissed him. ''Goodbye, Nick.''

He watched her walk to the door.

He watched her open it.

And then he watched her walk through it and out of his life.

Chapter Eleven

Kristin managed not to break down until she'd reached the safety of her car. She even managed to hang on until she'd started the Mazda and pulled away from the curb. But as soon as she was around the corner from Nick's house and sure that he could no longer see her, she pulled over to the side of the road, turned off the engine again, put her head down on the steering wheel and wept as if her heart would break.

She cried for a long time.

Nick, Nick...why? Why?

She cried until there were no more tears left, until she was weak and totally spent. Then, fishing a clean tissue out of her purse, she blew her nose, took a deep shuddering breath and headed for home.

She prayed everyone would be asleep when she

got there. Thankfully, the house was dark. It looked as if everyone had turned in for the night. She was so grateful, because if she'd had to face anyone, even Milly, she wasn't sure she could have managed it without Milly knowing something was terribly wrong.

She let herself into the quiet house and slowly climbed the stairs to her room. *This is just a momentary reprieve. You're going to have to face the family in the morning. So you'll have to be strong. No wallowing.*

Kristin forced back a fresh bout of tears. Crying solved nothing. Crying was self-indulgent. And she could not afford self-indulgence. Her life might have just blown up in her face, but she could not go through the remainder of it crying over what could never be.

Face it, Nick has chosen.

And his choice said clearly that there was no hope for the two of them.

Not now.

Not ever.

She must accept that…and move on.

Nick told himself he was better off without her.

If her family meant more to her than he did, he didn't want her. Hell, no. He wanted a woman who would put him first. Who, when there was a choice to be made, would always choose him.

And if Kristin couldn't do that, especially when she knew how her parents had betrayed her, then she certainly wasn't the woman for him.

As he charged around the small house like a caged bear, he told himself he was actually lucky he'd found out what she was really like before it was too late.

But no matter how many times he told himself he'd had a narrow escape and should be relieved instead of regretful, he still had an ache in his chest that refused to go away. And Kristin's sad eyes and her words, delivered with such despair, haunted him.

Until this moment, I thought I loved you, too. But now...I realize that I love the man you were, not the man you've become....

She was wrong, dammit!

Dead wrong.

But her insinuation that he was somehow less than honorable and a man she couldn't respect, gnawed at him.

He'd thought he had completely banished the feelings of inferiority that his growing-up years in Green River had produced, but her rejection of him reawakened all those old feelings.

Second-class. Trash. Son of a drunk. Like father, like son.

That night, he tossed and turned, unable to get comfortable no matter what he did. His mind refused to shut down. Over and over again, he replayed every word exchanged, every touch, every kiss, every image of Kristin from the past few days.

Sometime in the middle of the interminable night, he got up and walked to the window. He parted the drapes and stared out at the moon-washed street. The stately old homes and manicured yards seemed to mock him.

What was he doing here?

He didn't belong here.

He'd *never* belonged here.

For two cents, he would pack up his gear and go back to Manhattan tomorrow.

Kristin awakened with a dull headache and puffy eyes. She took one look at herself in the mirror and grimaced. A long, hot shower helped. So did cotton pads soaked in witch hazel, placed on her eyelids.

Once she was satisfied she could do nothing else to disguise the ravages of the previous day, she carefully made up her face, using foundation and concealer and more blush than she normally would. Finally, feeling she would pass inspection, she went downstairs.

Her mother was already seated at the breakfast table. She looked much better than she'd looked the day before. The circles under her eyes had all but disappeared. She even managed a cheerful smile. "Good morning, darling. I was hoping you'd be down soon. I'm anxious to get to the hospital as soon as possible."

"Have you talked to anyone there this morning?" Kristin said. She sat and poured herself a cup of coffee and glass of juice.

"Yes. I called first thing. The nurse said your father had a quiet night and was doing well."

"That's great news." Kristin returned her mother's smile, then served herself some of the fruit salad and warm blueberry muffins that were this morning's offering. She wasn't really hungry, but she knew she needed to eat.

"Did you sleep well?" her mother asked.

"I've had better nights," Kristin answered honestly.

"Darling..." Her mother hesitated. "Have you given any more thought to our conversation?"

"About breaking my engagement, you mean?"

"Yes." Worry clouded Meredith's eyes.

Kristin sighed, hating that she was adding to her mother's problems, even though so much of the present turmoil had been caused by her parents to begin with. "Yes, of course, I have."

"And?"

"I don't know."

"Kristin..."

"Look, I'm sorry. I wish I could promise you that everything was fine, but we both know it isn't. I'm just not sure what I'm going to do, but I will promise you one thing. I won't do or say anything to upset Daddy right now. Beyond that...well, I honestly don't know."

"I suppose I can't ask for more," her mother said slowly.

Kristin's eyes met her mother's. "No, Mother, you can't."

Just then Lindsay came bouncing into the room, so the subject was, of necessity, dropped. Kristin was glad to see that Lindsay, too, looked brighter today.

"Kris," Lindsay said, "did Mom tell you? Daddy's doing good this morning." Her dark eyes shone happily.

"Yes, honey, she did."

"Maybe now I can go to the hospital tonight." Lindsay looked hopefully at Meredith.

Meredith smiled across the table. "Yes. For sure tonight. I promise. Now, hurry up and eat some breakfast. The bus will be here in fifteen minutes."

"Okay."

Lindsay plopped down, filled her plate and ate, then skipped off to catch the school bus. By then Kristin and Meredith were finished, too, so they got ready to leave for the hospital.

Kristin was grateful that her mother did not raise the subject of her engagement again. But that didn't keep Kristin from thinking about her dilemma and what she was going to do now. Even though it wasn't going to work out between her and Nick as she'd hoped, she still felt she must come clean with Doug.

The big question was, after what had happened the previous night, did she still want to break her engagement? She knew she had to decide now, because after telling Doug, if he still wanted her, she had to know what her answer would be.

Maybe he'll tell you to get lost, and you'll have no choice.

Yes, maybe he would. But what if he didn't? Could she still marry him after what had happened? Did she want to?

If Doug still wants you after you tell him about Nick, you'd be a fool not to marry him.

Because regardless of the events of the past few days, nothing had really changed, had it?

Yes, she loved Nick, but her love for him was a hopeless love that would never bring her anything but heartache. And all the reasons why she'd originally accepted Doug's proposal still remained true.

She still wanted to be married. She still wanted to have children. And she was still tied to Green River by Lindsay, whom she would never leave.

If things had worked out between you and Nick, you would have had to leave Green River. Either that, or tell him about Lindsay. So everything has really worked out for the best....

Doug was a good man.

And when Nick went through with his threat to ruin her father, Doug would be there to help her and her family pick up the pieces.

By the time they reached the hospital, Kristin had made her decision.

After they'd talked, if Doug still wanted to marry her, the wedding would go forth as scheduled.

Wednesday was a much better day than Tuesday had been. Kristin's father was more alert and seemed stronger. He was glad to see them. Kristin and her mother, and later on, Brooke, took turns sitting with him.

When it was Kristin's turn to be alone with him, she prepared herself for the inevitable questions and accusations, but all her father said was, "Now you know what kind of man Nick Petrillo is."

Kristin had already decided that until her father

was stronger, she would simply agree with whatever he said, so she nodded, and her father seemed satisfied. But even though her father was only saying what she herself had said, she couldn't help thinking that if a person wanted to know why Nick was the way he was, that person wouldn't have to look any farther than this room.

"I got a call from Ted today. He said Jennifer's decided to come with him."

Kristin smiled. Ted Hoffman was Doug's college roommate and best friend. Jennifer was Ted's significant other. He'd been trying to get her to marry him for years, without success. "Good. It'll be nice to see her again."

Kristin and Doug were sitting in the hospital cafeteria, at a corner table near by back. It was past the most popular dinner hour, so there were relatively few people in the room. They had just finished eating and Kristin had been gearing herself to do what she had to do.

It was time to tell Doug everything.

She took a deep breath. "Doug," she said, "there's something I have to tell you. It…it won't be easy, so please bear with me."

Doug gave her a quizzical look. "You know you can tell me anything."

"Yes, I know. Okay. Here goes. When I was seventeen, I fell in love with a boy a few years older than me. I wanted to marry him, and he wanted to marry me. But my father disapproved of him—violently—so we planned to run away to New York together.''

Doug smiled indulgently, as if to say *We were all silly kids once.*

Kristin plowed on doggedly. ''But Dad found out what we were planning, and he figured out a way to stop us.'' As she explained what had happened, she left out Nick's name and simply referred to him as ''the boy.''

''Well,'' Doug said when she'd finished with that part, ''I understand how your father felt, and even though what he did was underhanded, I really can't blame him.'' His eyes were kind as they met hers. ''How do you feel about what he did?''

''I only found out the whole story a couple of days ago, and I was pretty upset.''

''I can understand that, too, but you're not *still* upset, are you? After all, that all happened a long time ago.''

''There's more,'' she said, evading his question. ''I haven't told you the whole story.'' It was hard for her to meet Doug's eyes, but she did. ''The boy? He...he came back to Green River last week.''

Slowly, comprehension dawned in Doug's eyes. ''Nick Petrillo,'' he murmured.

''Yes.''

He nodded, face sober, eyes thoughtful. ''Now things begin to fall in place. It's because of what happened between the two of you that he's been buying up stock in the company, isn't it?''

''Yes.''

''Do you think he's planning a takeover?''

Kristin nodded. "Yes."

Doug thought for a while, then reached across the table and took her hand. "Listen, Kristin, I don't want you or your mother to worry about this. I'll look into it. I'll talk to Petrillo. Surely he can be reasoned with. As I said, what happened happened a long time ago."

"No, believe me, Doug, that's *not* a good idea. Besides, you don't know everything. The thing is, I..." She swallowed. "God, this is hard." Taking a deep breath, she continued. "Something happened between Nick and me, after his return, that might make you not want to have anything more to do with me."

He frowned.

Kristin allowed a moment or two to pass, then said, "I went over to see Nick the other night after you and I had dinner with your parents. We... I spent the night with him."

Doug stared at her. "You mean...you slept with him?"

Kristin nodded. "I—I'm sorry, Doug. I never meant to hurt you."

"You never meant to hurt me! How the hell did you *think* I'd feel?" He yanked his hand away and stood. His face, normally so genial, was set in tight lines.

"Doug...please..." Kristin stood, too, reaching out to touch his arm.

But he shook her off. Then, without a backward glance, he stalked out of the room. By the time Kristin reached the outer hallway, there was no sign of him.

That night, Kristin lay awake a long time. She had made a royal mess of her life. She had lost Nick. And now she'd lost Doug, too.

She turned her engagement ring round and round on her finger. Tomorrow she would return it. And then, somehow, she would have to find a way to break the news to her father that there would be no wedding.

But the following morning, early, Doug called.

"Listen," he said, "I've done a lot of thinking since yesterday. We need to talk. Can you meet me for breakfast before you go to the hospital?"

"Of course."

An hour and fifteen minutes later, they were seated across from each other in a booth at the local Denny's. With a pang, Kristin realized Doug had had as sleepless a night as she'd had, if his red-rimmed eyes were any indication.

"Tell me one thing," Doug said after the waitress had come and gone. "Are you in love with Petrillo?"

"I...thought I was."

"But you no longer think so?"

"What I think doesn't really matter. This thing between Nick and me—it will never work. It's over, for good this time."

"So you're not going to see him again?"

"No."

Doug nodded, giving her a long, thoughtful look. "Good, because I think he's been using you."

"Using me!"

"Yes. Don't you see? It's all part of his plan to get back at your father. He must know your father has handpicked me to succeed him as the president of Blair."

"But Doug, there was no *plan* for Nick and I to…" She lowered her voice. "Sleep together. It…it just *happened*."

Doug smiled knowingly. "Things don't just *happen* where someone like Petrillo is concerned."

"How can you say that? You don't even know him."

"And you do?"

Kristin sank back against the booth. Even though she was certain Doug's reasoning was completely off base, how could she honestly say she knew Nick? This Nick, the one who'd come to Green River, bore little resemblance to the man she'd known and loved.

"He also wanted to humiliate me," Doug said.

Kristin wanted to say she was sure Nick hadn't given Doug a passing thought. After all, *she* had hardly thought of him. But she had hurt Doug enough.

"Yesterday, when you told me what happened," Doug continued, "were you intending to break our engagement?"

"I didn't really have a plan. I—I figured that would be your decision to make."

He nodded again. "Well, I don't want to call off our wedding. I don't want to give that son of a bitch the satisfaction of knowing he ruined our plans."

Ruined our *plans?* What about our *lives?* "Are you sure, Doug?"

"Hell, yes, I'm sure."

Kristin wondered why she didn't feel more of a sense of relief. What was wrong with her? She should be jumping up and down with joy that he'd managed to get past his anger of yesterday. So what if he'd rationalized events to his satisfaction? Did it really matter?

Later, as she recalled their conversation, she couldn't help thinking how different Doug and Nick were. She couldn't imagine Nick reacting as Doug had if the situations were reversed. He'd have been so furious, he'd have marched over to Doug's house and punched him in the nose.

Yes, but she also couldn't imagine Doug ever doing anything to hurt her or her family, the way Nick planned to.

Count your blessings, she told herself sternly. *And don't wish for things you can't have.*

For the next week, Kristin divided her time between the hospital and taking care of the last-minute details of the wedding. Each day, her father improved. And each day, her wedding came closer.

On Monday, just five days before the wedding would take place, Dr. Palmer said her father could go home. "But remember," he cautioned Meredith, "no excitement, see that he eats right, takes his medicine and gets plenty of rest. And bring him to my office in a week so I can check his progress."

"But Simon, Kristin's wedding is this weekend,"

Meredith said. "Are you saying we should postpone it?"

"No, no, that would get Edmond all upset. He's really happy about the upcoming wedding. No, I think it's best if you go ahead as scheduled, just do your best to get him to take it easy."

Following the doctor's orders was easier said than done.

"What does that quack mean by saying I can't go back to work?" Edmond raged on Tuesday, his second day home.

"He's not a quack," Meredith answered mildly. "He's the best cardiac man in the area, and you know it. Besides, Simon is more than your doctor. He's your friend. And if he says you must take it easy until you're completely well, then that's what you'll do."

"I feel fine," Edmond muttered. "Quit coddling me, Meredith."

He continued to grumble and complain, but Kristin's mother held firm. He was not going to the office until Dr. Palmer said he could.

But on one point, Edmond wouldn't budge. He planned to attend the stockholders' meeting Friday morning, no matter what Meredith or anyone else said.

Mention of the stockholders' meeting caused Kristin's stomach to hollow out in fear, but her father didn't seem afraid at all. "Silas says that even though Petrillo has a larger number of shares than anyone else," he told her and her mother, "he doesn't have enough to take control of the company, which is what we were afraid of. Silas has polled all the stockholders who are attending. They've agreed to vote with me. If we hang tough, we'll beat that bastard.''

Kristin wasn't so sure. She couldn't imagine anyone beating Nick now. But she didn't contradict her father. What would be the point? She also didn't tell her mother her fears. Again, what would be the point?

Instead, she worried silently. How would her father handle it if things didn't go his way at the meeting? *Could* he handle it?

Oh, God. Maybe she should have told Nick about Lindsay. If he knew Lindsay was his daughter, it might have made all the difference, for surely Nick wouldn't want to bring ruin upon his daughter's head.

But she couldn't use Lindsay as a club against Nick. Besides, maybe knowing about her would change nothing in his eyes. In fact, maybe if he knew about Lindsay, he would just be angrier and more determined than ever to exact his revenge against her father because he would have more reason to do so.

There was nothing Kristin could do.

Except wait...and pray.

Nick spent the days after Kristin's last visit to him in a set routine. Mornings, before breakfast, he ran at least five miles. Then he'd go back to the house, shower, dress, eat something light, then spend the rest of the day working via his computer, modem and fax.

As part of his preparation for the stockholders' meeting on Friday, he read the minutes of the last four meetings and tried to identify and study the personalities of all the major players at Blair.

Each evening he ate dinner at D'Amato's. Afterward, he would stop at the video store and rent a couple of movies to help pass the evening hours.

He carefully kept his mind off Kristin and focused on the objective at hand.

One week after Kristin had walked out on him, he decided it was time to play his next-to-last card before the meeting. On Wednesday morning, he picked up the phone and called Jacob Winesap, a state senator whose wife had inherited a large chunk of Blair Manufacturing stock and was one of the major shareholders, although her husband always voted her stock for her.

"Who's calling, please?" said a slightly nasal female voice.

"My name will be meaningless to the senator," Nick said smoothly. "Just tell him I'm a fellow stockholder in Blair Manufacturing and must speak to him on a matter of importance concerning the upcoming shareholders' meeting."

"One moment, please."

A few minutes later, an irritated-sounding Jacob Winesap said a curt "Hello?"

"Senator Winesap. My name is Nick Petrillo. I'm a major shareholder of Blair Manufacturing—"

"Yes, yes," Winesap said impatiently, "my secretary told me all that. What can I do for you, Mr. Petrillo? This is a very busy day for me. I've got—"

"I recently purchased two promissory notes signed by you," Nick cut in. "We need to discuss them."

There was absolute silence for several long moments. "That's impossible," Winesap finally said.

"What's impossible? That I purchased the notes or a discussion between us?"

"You couldn't have purchased any notes of mine."

"Senator Winesap, if I hadn't purchased the notes from Capital Trust, how would I even *know* about them?"

"B-but," Winesap sputtered, "Ross Dennison *assured* me those notes wouldn't be sold."

"Ross Dennison is no longer the president of Capital, and the new president has other ideas about the best way to serve his shareholders."

Another long moment passed. Then, in a much more conciliatory voice, Winesap said, "When would you like to meet?"

"Today," Nick said.

"Today! I've got a full agenda for the rest of the week. I can't see you today. In fact, the earliest I could meet with you is next Tuesday."

Nick hardened his voice. "Today."

There was a heavy sigh from the other end of the phone. "Fine, fine. Let me look at my appointments. Okay. Be here at one. I can give you a half hour. No more."

If he had wanted six hours of Winesap's time, Winesap would have had no choice but to oblige him. But Nick didn't contradict the older man. He'd won his point. He could afford to be generous.

Promptly at one, Nick presented himself to Winesap's secretary, who turned out to be a whippet-thin brunette with eyes too green to be real—colored contact lenses, Nick figured—and the reddest lipstick he'd ever seen.

"I'll tell the senator you're here," she said, giving him a brilliant smile.

Winesap kept him waiting fifteen minutes. Nick smothered a smile. The power games men played were nothing new to him.

"What's this all about?" the senator said when Nick was finally ushered in and they'd disposed of the formalities of shaking hands and pretending to be friendly.

Nick let a few seconds pass while he studied the older man. Tall, well-built, with thick silvery hair and dark eyes, Winesap radiated an arrogance and sense of entitlement Nick had seen many times before with men who occupied powerful positions. "What it's about is I've decided to call in your notes."

Winesap's handsome face drained of color. "You...you can't do that."

"Oh?"

"I—I have five years to pay those notes."

"You *did* have five years to pay them."

Winesap's Adam's apple bobbed as he swallowed. He licked his lips.

"If," Nick continued implacably, "you met the payments on time." He opened his briefcase, withdrew copies of the notes and handed them across

Winesap's large, mahogany desk. "A payment was due September 15. You didn't make it."

Winesap's hand trembled as he took the papers. "I—I'm a little strapped for cash right now."

Nick shrugged.

"If...if you'd just give me some time..."

"Sorry. I haven't got any time."

"But what good would calling in the notes do you?" Winesap said. "If I don't have the money, I don't have it."

"Have you forgotten you put up your wife's stock in Blair Manufacturing as collateral on the notes?" Nick said softly. He saw the fear leap into Winesap's eyes. Nick waited while the knowledge sank in that he, and not Winesap, was in full control of the situation. Then, and only then, did he add, "There *is* a way out of this. A way where your wife will never have to know what you did. A way where I will forget about calling in your notes before their due date."

Winesap swallowed again. "Wh-what is it?"

"All you have to do is vote the same way I vote at Friday's shareholders' meeting."

Like a drowning man, Winesap grasped at the lifeline Nick had thrown him. As Nick drove back to Green River from Hartford, he wondered why he didn't feel a greater sense of satisfaction. Victory over Edmond Blair was nearly his. He had expected to feel great triumph.

Instead, he just felt tired. He would be glad when the meeting on Friday was over. All he really wanted now was to leave Green River, forget about Kristin and get on with his life.

Chapter Twelve

"Kris, what's wrong? You've been so unhappy the past few days. Are you still worried about Dad?"

Kristin looked up. Brooke's sympathetic eyes met hers across the lunch table. The sisters were having lunch after spending the morning at their favorite salon, where each had had a hair trimming, manicure and pedicure in preparation for Kristin's wedding. "I'm sorry. I'm such a pathetic mess."

"No, you're not! And don't be sorry. It's just that I want to help if I can."

Kristin sighed. "Yes, I'm worried about Dad, but not in the way you think."

"Well, what then? C'mon, tell me." Brooke took a bite of her chicken salad.

So Kristin told her everything. About going to Nick's. About what happened between them. About coming home and discovering their father had had the heart attack. About finding out later, from Silas Guthrie, that Nick had purchased large blocks of stock in Blair Manufacturing. And then about the confrontation between her and Nick and its outcome.

"Oh, Kris," Brooke said when her sister had finally wound down. "How awful for you. Gee, I'm so sorry."

Kristin nodded. "Me, too. I just wish..." She laughed ruefully. "But there's no use wishing, is there?" Kristin concentrated on her tuna melt and fought the depression that had been a constant companion the past week. "I'm so afraid of what's going to happen tomorrow at the stockholders' meeting. Daddy says there's nothing to worry about, that he has enough votes to beat Nick at whatever game he's playing, but he doesn't know Nick the way I do. I think Nick will win, and it scares me half to death to think what will happen to Daddy if he does. Oh, God, Brooke, what if Daddy has another heart attack? I wish now I'd never told Nick what really happened twelve years ago."

"But how would that have changed anything? He still would have gone to the stockholders' meeting prepared to ruin Daddy."

"I know, I know." That was the trouble. She *did* know. But she still kept thinking there must have been something she could have done...or not done...to change what she knew was going to happen.

"Kris? Have...have you considered telling Nick about Lindsay?"

Kristin's heart skipped. "Yes, but each time I do, I still come to the same conclusion. I don't think knowing about Lindsay would make Nick feel kindlier toward Daddy and it would be taking a terrible chance with Lindsay's well-being and security. I just can't do that."

Brooke was silent for a long time. Then, softly, she said, "But don't you think he has a right to know?"

Kristin nodded. Even though she had told herself she wouldn't cry over Nick again, there was a lump in her throat. "Yes. That's one of the things that's tearing me to pieces. I do think he has a right to know. But Lindsay has rights, too. And her rights have to take precedence over his."

"But Kris, don't you think—"

"Listen," Kristin said, interrupting. "I've agonized about all of this so much, it makes my head hurt to think about it. I've gone round and round, but the outcome is always the same. If I were certain he wouldn't use the information about Lindsay to hurt Daddy or to try to take Lindsay away from Daddy and Mother and me, then I'd tell him. But I can't be certain. He's changed so much, Brooke. He seems so hard. I have no idea how he'd react if he knew, and I just can't gamble where Lindsay's welfare is concerned."

"But Kris, he couldn't take Lindsay away from Daddy and Mother. Could he?"

"I don't know, but even if he couldn't, the whole mess would become public. Lindsay would know her entire life was a lie. Don't you think that would disrupt her life?''

Brooke grimaced. ''You're right, of course. I guess I hadn't thought about that aspect of it.''

''Believe me, I've thought about every *possible* aspect of the situation. I told you. I've thought so much, my head hurts.''

''It's all so *unfair*, though,'' Brooke said. ''Nick is hurting, you're hurting, Daddy and Mother are hurting and Doug...what about Doug? If only I hadn't told Mother about you and Nick, none of this would have happened. You and Nick would have been married for years, and the two of you would be raising Lindsay.''

Brooke looked so woebegone, Kristin felt sorry for her. She reached across the table and patted Brooke's hand. ''Oh, Brooke, quit blaming yourself. You were just a kid. You couldn't have known what was going to happen.''

''I know, but I can't help blaming myself. I mean, things are such a *mess!* And I just wish I could think of something to do to make everything come out all right.''

Kristin shook her head sadly. ''Thank you for caring, but I've faced it. There's nothing anyone can do.''

Thursday afternoon dragged by. Nick couldn't seem to settle down to anything. About three o'clock, he decided to go for a long drive—anything to help the hours pass until tomorrow morning's board meeting.

He was already outside, walking toward the garage, when a black BMW pulled into the driveway.

He watched as Brooke Morris climbed awkwardly out of the driver's seat and walked toward him. Nick hadn't seen Kristin's younger sister since the night of the symphony benefit, and he was struck anew with the resemblance between her and Kristin. In fact, all three sisters looked alike, he thought, remembering Lindsay, the youngest, with a smile of pleasure.

"Hi, Nick," Brooke said. "You getting ready to go somewhere?"

He shrugged. "Nowhere important."

"Do you think we could talk for a few minutes?"

"Sure. Let's go inside where we can sit down."

She gave him a grateful smile. "Thanks. At this stage of my *development*—" she patted her rounded stomach "—sitting down is infinitely preferable to standing."

Once they were inside and seated in the living room, Nick offered her a soft drink.

"A glass of water would be lovely," she said. A few minutes later, water glass in hand, she gave him a level look. "I suppose you know why I'm here."

Although he had a pretty strong idea what her reason was, he shrugged and said, "Not really."

"I'm here to beg you to reconsider what you're planning to do to my father, to our family, tomorrow at the stockholders' meeting."

She looked so earnest and so worried, Nick felt a momentary regret, which he quickly banished. "I'm sorry, but I can't."

"This will do more than hurt my father, you know. It'll also hurt Kristin."

"Kristin made her choice."

"Maybe she had less of a choice than you know."

"Look," Nick said, "I appreciate what you're trying to do. You love your family, and you don't want to see anything bad happen to any of them. But your father has brought this on himself. He made some poor financial decisions and sold stock he never should have sold if he wanted to remain in control of the company. What I'm planning is just sound business strategy. As the new major stockholder in the company, I want a man with sound financial judgment in charge so that my investment will be protected."

Her big eyes, so like Kristin's, met his. "We both know this isn't about protecting your investment. This is a personal vendetta."

Nick shrugged. "Your father started this war, not me."

"But this isn't just between the two of you. There are other people involved. Innocent people who don't deserve to be caught in the cross fire."

"In a war, there are always casualties."

She sighed, closing her eyes briefly. She seemed to be struggling with something. "What my father did to you all those years ago," she finally said, "it was terrible—I'll be the first to admit it. But he was only trying to protect Kristin from what he perceived as a threat to her well-being. Can't you understand that? Can't you…forgive that? If you had a child, wouldn't you want to protect her…or him…from harm?'' She touched her stomach. ''Wouldn't you do anything in your power to keep her safe and happy?''

''Yes, of course,'' Nick said impatiently, ''but I—''

''There's something you should know,'' she said, breaking in. ''Something someone should tell you that I know would make a difference.''

''Look,'' he said, ''there's nothing you can say that's going to make any difference, so don't waste your breath. Go home, Brooke. This doesn't concern you. It isn't your fight.''

She stared at him. It was very quiet in the room. After a long moment, she sighed wearily. ''You're right. It's not my fight. I shouldn't have come here. Please forgive me.'' Carefully placing her water glass on the coffee table, she levered herself up from the couch. ''I'm sorry for the role I played twelve years ago, Nick. I wish we could turn back the clock and do it all again. Maybe this time we'd get it right.''

Friday morning Kristin awakened to the sound of rain. Great, she thought. Just great. A gray day to match her gray mood.

She was dreading the day. This, the day before her wedding, should be one of the most exciting days of her life. Instead, it might turn out to be one of the worst.

The stockholders' meeting would convene at ten. Yesterday, she and her mother had discussed it and decided that the whole family, Lindsay included, would be there as moral support for her father.

Breakfast was a quiet affair, with everyone lost in their own thoughts. Even Lindsay seemed subdued, as if she'd picked up on the underlying tension.

At nine o'clock, Kristin joined her family in the downstairs hall. Edmond had said he wanted to get to the meeting early. Kristin studied her father surreptitiously as they prepared to leave. Although her father looked better than he'd looked a week ago, she could still see the ravages of his recent illness in the new lines around his eyes and mouth, the paleness of his skin and his almost-hesitant gait. This evidence of his mortality saddened her. Somehow, she'd always thought of her father as invincible, but in the days since Nick's return to Green River, she'd learned just how vulnerable Edmond was.

"Are we all ready?" her mother said, straightening the jacket of her cherry red Chanel suit.

As ready as I'll ever be, Kristin thought. She smiled down at Lindsay, who looked adorable in a short green dress and matching tights.

Twenty minutes later, they were ushered into the large conference room where the stockholders' meeting would take place. The officers of the company would sit at the head table. The other attendees would sit in the sixty-odd chairs set up theater-style.

There were already about a dozen early arrivals, with more arriving all the time. Kristin looked around. She recognized most of the faces. Nick wasn't there yet. She was glad. She needed some time to get her emotions under control.

Her father headed straight for the head table, where he and Silas Guthrie and Doug, who looked up and smiled at her, immediately began to confer in low tones.

Kristin, Lindsay and her mother walked to the first row of chairs and sat down. Kristin placed her purse between the two empty chairs next to her, saving places for Brooke and Chandler. *United we stand, united we'll fall,* Kristin thought wryly. She turned slightly in her chair so she could watch the entrance. She wanted to know when Nick arrived. She hardly acknowledged the tiny hope buried deep that maybe, just maybe, he'd had a change of heart and wouldn't be there.

Her hope was short-lived. About ten minutes later, he walked through the door. For an instant, she couldn't breathe. The sight of him, so tall and darkly handsome, looking the very picture of success and confidence, hurt her so deeply, it was like someone had plunged a knife into her chest. She had to fight to keep her face calm, fight to keep from giving way to the emotions pummeling her.

She knew she should turn around.

She knew it was dangerous to look at him.

She knew, from the way his gaze swept the room, that at any moment, their eyes would meet.

But she couldn't look away.

Nick saw her immediately.

He'd thought he was prepared. But as always, the sight of her caused his chest to constrict. She looked incredibly beautiful sitting there in her black wool suit, her slender legs crossed. She was looking at him, too, and for a few seconds, they might have been the only two people in the room.

Then a man Nick didn't recognize walked up to her and said something, and she began to talk to him and faced forward again.

Nick took in a deep breath and walked toward the front of the room, but on the opposite end from the Blairs. It was then that he saw Edmond Blair for the first time. Nick was shocked. Of course, he'd known Edmond had had a heart attack, but he'd never expected to see this kind of change in the man. Why, Kristin's father looked ten years older than the last time they'd seen each other.

He's an old man. A sick, old man....

While Nick was still grappling with the discovery that his hated adversary had somehow bested him, Edmond looked up. Some of his old fire hardened his face, and he glared at Nick.

At that precise moment, a young voice piped, "Nick! Hi! I didn't know you were going to be here."

Nick turned. A smiling Lindsay stood there, dark eyes bright with pleasure. "Well, hello," he said. "I didn't know you were going to be here, either."

"I shouldn't be. I had to skip school, but Mom said it would be okay, just this once," Lindsay confided. "She said it was important for the whole family to come and give my dad moral support." Her smiled faded a bit and she bit her lip in consternation. "My dad's been sick, you know."

Looking down into those eyes that were so eerily

like his mother's, Nick felt a hot rush of shame engulf him. "Yes, I know."

"He scared me," Lindsay continued, "that night when he had his heart attack."

Nick swallowed. He couldn't think of a thing to say.

"I hope he won't get sick again."

"I hope not, either."

Then, in that way that children have, her mood abruptly changed, and her troubled expression was replaced with another happy grin. "I told my teacher what you said about me coming to New York and seeing the stock exchange. She was so excited about it." She frowned slightly. "You haven't changed your mind, have you?"

"No," Nick said, "I haven't changed my mind." But he couldn't imagine Kristin or any other member of her family wanting Lindsay to have anything to do with him after today.

"Oh, good," she said. "'Cause I really, really want to come." Her grin was innocent and totally guileless. "Well, I'd better go back to my seat before Mom has a fit. She didn't want me to get up and come over here. See you later."

She skipped off, and Nick sat down. By now it was nine-fifty and almost all the seats were filled, not only in the body of the room, but around the head table. A buzz of voices filled the room.

Nick, trying to ignore the guilt that Lindsay's comments had produced, studied the men seated at the head table. His eyes met those of Jacob Winesap, who quickly looked away, but not before Nick saw the flash of guilt in Winesap's eyes.

Suddenly, the shame that seeing Lindsay and hearing her concern about her father's health had produced, hit him full force. *What in the hell am I doing here?*

Once more, he looked at Edmond Blair. At how frail and weak he seemed. He thought about what an uneven contest the next hour would be. The thought gave him no pleasure.

Then Nick's gaze swung to Meredith Blair, and he saw the concern in her eyes as she watched her husband.

Next he looked at Brooke, who met his gaze for an instant before looking away.

Beside Brooke was Kristin, who kept her face turned away from him. Her beloved profile made his heart ache for all the lost dreams.

Last he looked at Lindsay. She was such a sweet kid. Just the kind of kid he'd like to have. Filled with hope and enthusiasm. A kid whose secure life would soon be rocked to its core.

For the first time, the things Kristin, and then Brooke, had said to him, really had meaning.

If he went ahead with his plan to oust Edmond Blair and take over Blair Manufacturing, he would not only destroy Edmond, he would destroy the security and happiness of the entire family.

Kristin told him she loved the man he once was, not the man he'd become. She also told him they could never have built any happiness on the ashes of her family.

She was right.

About everything.

Nick stood. He walked over to the table that held the proxies. He hurriedly filled one out, signed his name and then, ignoring the eyes of everyone else, walked over to Kristin. Her startled gaze met his.

He tried to smile. "This is a wedding gift," he said. "I...hope you'll be very happy. You deserve to be."

He thrust the proxy into her hands, and then, before he could change his mind, he walked out.

Kristin stared at the proxy. Her heart was beating so fast and so hard, she was sure everyone could hear it. Her hands shook as she lifted the paper.

What did this mean?

This is a wedding gift. I...hope you'll be very happy. You deserve to be.

As her eyes focused on the numbers Nick had filled in on the proxy form, she realized he had signed over his voting rights to every share of stock he owned.

Every share.

Why?

What had caused him to change his mind?

Suddenly, the import of what had just happened really hit her, and she was filled with the most incredible relief. She looked up. The eyes of everyone in her family were on her. Silas Guthrie and Doug were both watching her, too.

Slowly she got up and walked to the head table. Brooke and her mother followed her.

"What happened?" her father said. "What did he say to you?"

"He...he gave me his proxy. For all his shares."

Her mother gasped. "Oh, thank God."

Brooke murmured, "Well, I'll be darned."

Silas Guthrie smiled.

Doug grinned.

"I told you we'd beat him," Edmond said, beaming and putting his arm around Doug's shoulders. "Well, son, it looks like you're a shoo-in to be the next president of Blair. It also looks like Nick Petrillo is finally out of our lives."

Chapter Thirteen

Nick drove straight to the Longwell house. Keeping his mind carefully blank, he walked inside, quickly rounded up and packed all his belongings, then carried the bags out to the car.

Once they were securely stowed, he went back inside and checked everything to make sure the house was tidy and he hadn't forgotten anything.

Satisfied, he called Albritton Realty and asked for Glenda.

"Hey," she said, "how have things been going? You enjoying your stay in our fair city?"

Nick heard the smile in her voice and smiled, too. "Yes, but I'm afraid it's over. In fact, that's why I'm calling. I've concluded my business here, and I'm ready to head back to New York. Is it okay with you if I just leave the key to the house under the back doormat or do I need to bring it by the office?''

''Well, as much as I'd enjoy seeing you again, it's not necessary to make a trip over here. Just leave the key under the doormat. I'll stop by on my way to lunch and pick it up.''

''Thanks.''

''Maybe if I get to New York sometime, I'll give you a call.''

''I'd like that.''

They said their goodbyes and hung up.

Ten minutes later, as Nick accelerated onto the main highway, he passed a sign that read: You Are Now Leaving Green River. Come Back Soon.

Although the board meeting was long over and Kristin was now getting dressed to attend the rehearsal dinner, she was still in a state of confusion—almost disbelief—over the morning's development.

What had convinced Nick not to take over the company?

This was the question that had nagged at her ever since he'd so abruptly given her his proxy.

Was it something Lindsay had said to him?

Or was it something else?

Kristin desperately wanted to believe he had finally realized he loved her too much to hurt her this way. But if he loved her, then why had he walked out without saying something about seeing her again?

He *did* say something.

This is a wedding gift. I...hope you'll be very happy. You deserve to be.

A wedding gift.

Tomorrow is your wedding. Yours and Doug's.

Kristin sank onto the side of her bed and stared into space. Oh, God, how had her life gotten into such a mess? How had she ended up engaged to a man she didn't love while the man she *did* love had been lost to her twice?

But, really, what did it matter? she thought hopelessly. What did any of it matter?

Maybe Nick had been right to begin with. Maybe it *was* too late for them. Maybe there were just too many insurmountable problems for them to ever have any kind of future together. Maybe, the day she went along with the fiction that Lindsay was her sister, she had sealed her fate. And his.

She wondered again if she should have told Nick about Lindsay. She knew now that he would not have used that knowledge against her.

Sighing deeply, she eyed the telephone. She even stood up and walked over to where it sat. Put her hand on the receiver. Her heart pounded. Then, abruptly, she pulled her hand away.

What in God's name did she think she was doing? Doug would be there in less than ten minutes to take her to the rehearsal dinner. Did she *really* want to open this can of worms now?

Face it, Kristin. You made your decision. Now grit your teeth, quit feeling sorry for yourself and go downstairs and wait for your fiancé. And forget about Nick Petrillo!

* * *

Nick had gotten back to Manhattan in the middle of the afternoon. After unpacking, he'd briefly toyed with the idea of going to the office for a couple of hours, then decided the hell with it—the office and everything there could wait until Monday. He just wasn't in the mood to think about work.

Instead, he stripped out of his traveling clothes, donned his sweats and headed for his gym.

Two hours later, feeling marginally better after a vigorous session with the weights and machines, followed by a steam bath and swim, he headed back to his apartment and tried to decide how he wanted to spend the evening.

While mulling it over, he sorted through his accumulated mail and fought to keep his thoughts from straying to Kristin.

Although he'd been successful in keeping his mind occupied with something other than her for most of the day, this time he couldn't stop himself.

Her image haunted him.

The way she'd looked sitting there at the board meeting, staring up at him, was burned into his brain.

Why hadn't he said something to her? Something other than wishing her well? Why hadn't he at least made an attempt to find out if there was still hope for them?

His shoulders sagged wearily.

You're such a damned, stupid fool. You could have had her. All you would've had to do was agree to drop your vendetta against her father when she asked you to. If you'd done that, she would have called off her wedding and she'd be here with you now.

Instead, he'd lost her.

And tomorrow she would marry another man.

And Nick would be left with the bleak task of trying to figure out how he was going to live the rest of his life without her.

The rehearsal dinner was being held at the Lantern Inn, a quaint turn-of-the-century restaurant that had been a favorite of well-heeled Green Riverites for decades.

Tucked into a densely forested area near the place where the Green River turned south and headed toward its eventual destination of Long Island Sound, the inn had gotten its name from the dozens of lanterns flanking its mammoth doors, lining the surrounding walkways and hanging from nearby trees.

Kristin tried her best to be attentive and responsive to Doug's conversation on the twenty-five-minute drive to the restaurant. He was ebullient and said more than once how pleased he was with the way everything had turned out. It was all Kristin could do to smile enthusiastically and echo his sentiments.

And if he talked more about his plans for the company than he did about their personal future together, so what? She told herself she'd always known he was practical, so why was she feeling so discontented at this late date? After all, he wasn't the one who had changed. She was.

Even so, she was grateful when they reached the restaurant and she no longer had any time to think amid the flurry of hellos and hugs and the pleasant bustle of getting everyone seated.

Now they were about midway through the dinner. Her initial relief had worn off, and she was exhausted with the strain of having to pretend to be a happy bride. Praying she could make it through the evening without arousing anyone's concern or suspicion, she toyed with her food, pushing it around her plate to make it look as if she were eating it, even though she had no appetite. In fact, she felt queasy and was afraid if she *did* eat, it wouldn't stay down.

"How's your filet, darling?"

"Oh," Kristin said, turning to Doug, who sat on her left. "It's wonderful."

He eyed her plate. "You're not eating much of it."

"I know." She forced a chuckle. "I'm just nervous, I guess."

"Wedding jitters," Brooke pronounced. "I couldn't eat a thing at my rehearsal dinner."

Kristin gave her a grateful smile.

"But she's been making up for it ever since," Chandler said, laughing and ducking when Brooke made a fist and pretended she was going to punch him.

"I'm eating for two," she said primly.

"I know, honey, I'm just teasing you." Chandler leaned over and kissed her cheek.

Brooke patted his face.

The affectionate gestures and the expression of love on both their faces hurt to look at. Kristin blinked twice, too close to tears for comfort.

Hurry. Think about something else...think about something else....

After a moment, she'd gotten herself under control again. She took a small bite of her potatoes, and glanced over at the next table. Her father, sitting next to Bill Llewellyn, was laughing and talking expansively. He looked much better tonight, she thought. Better than he'd looked since his heart attack. Kristin was sure the absence of stress regarding Nick had more to do with the improvement than anything else.

Her mother looked happy, too.

Everyone is happy but me....

She fought the self-pitying thought. She knew if she gave way to her misery, she would be in grave danger of making a complete fool of herself.

Come on, Kristin. Get a grip.

Ted, the best man, chose that moment to rise to make a toast. He lifted his champagne glass.

"To my best friend, Doug," he said, "who has always known exactly what he wants and how to get it, and to his beautiful bride-to-be, Kristin...." He turned to smile at her, his open freckled face filled with goodwill. "I wish you both a long and happy life together."

Somehow, Kristin returned his smile.

Somehow, she drank the toast.

Somehow, she smiled and endured and made it

through the rest of the meal and the other toasts and well wishes that seemed to go on forever.

She played her role well enough so that no one seemed to realize anything was wrong.

And finally, the end of the evening was in sight. The dessert dishes were cleared away, and people began to mingle again in preparation for leaving.

Doug put his arm around her and leaned closer. "Darling, Ted wants to go outside to have a cigarette. Do you mind if I go with him?"

"No, of course not."

The sense of relief she felt when Doug walked out of the room frightened her. This was the man she would promise to love, honor and cherish tomorrow afternoon. This was the man she would live with for the rest of her life.

Suddenly, the enormity of what she was doing nearly overwhelmed her. Panic, worse than any she'd felt before, rolled over her like a thick cloud.

"Kris?" Brooke slipped her hand around Kristin's waist and squeezed. "Are you okay? You look like you might faint."

Kristin closed her eyes and swayed against Brooke.

"Breathe deeply," Brooke said in a low, urgent voice. "C'mon, take deep breaths. That's it." As she talked, she steered Kristin toward the ladies' room. "Nerves. It's just nerves. She's all right," she said as people began to notice what was happening.

Once inside the ladies' room, Brooke locked the door and checked under the stalls to make sure they were alone, while Kristin rinsed her face with cold water and tried to still her trembling hands and equally trembling heart. She breathed deeply as Brooke had instructed, and after a few minutes, she did feel better.

"Are you okay now?" Brooke said.

"I—I think so."

Their eyes met in the mirror.

"Kris, why don't you call him?"

Kristin looked down.

"You know you want to."

"Yes," Kristin whispered.

"Then why don't you?"

"I..." She took a deep breath before raising her eyes to meet her sister's. "It's too late."

Brooke's answer was quiet, but it seemed to ring in the room for a long time. "Is it?"

During the drive home, Kristin couldn't stop thinking about her sister's question. *Is it really too late?* A tiny seed of hope began to bloom.

Maybe it *wasn't.*

The number at the Longwell house rang and rang. Ten times. Twenty times.

There was no answer.

Kristin quietly replaced the receiver.

She tried the number again at midnight.

There was still no answer.

Again at one, no one picked up.

And at two.

At three o'clock, Kristin finally faced the truth.

She'd waited too long.

Nick was gone.

She cried herself to sleep.

Nick hit every bar he knew, and then some.

"Hey, Nick, you're really tyin' one on tonight," said Johnny, the bartender at King George's, a pseudo-English pub on West 59th.

"It's called drowning your sorrows," Nick said glumly. He drained his glass.

Johnny nodded sagely. "Gonna have a bad head in the morning."

"Yep."

That was the objective.

If his head hurt badly enough, he would not have to think about how much his heart ached.

The alarm went off at seven-thirty.

Moaning, Nick groped for it, finally locating the On/Off button. His head felt like twenty elephants were stomping on it.

For a few seconds after the intrusive jangle stopped, he thought it was a weekday morning. It wasn't until he'd stumbled out of bed and into the bathroom that he realized it was Saturday morning, and he hadn't needed to get up this early.

"Hell," he muttered, "you must have *really* been tanked last night if you turned on the alarm." He halfway thought about going back to bed, but he had the granddaddy of all hangovers and his head was throbbing so badly, he wasn't sure he could get back to sleep.

Instead, he splashed water on his face, then padded out to the kitchen to put on the coffee.

Several cups of coffee and several aspirins later, he stood under the shower and let the hot water pelt his body and thought about what was going to take place at five-thirty that evening.

"Why are you torturing yourself?" he muttered. "Don't think about it."

He soaped himself and tried to turn his thoughts to the day and what he would do to get through it.

But his traitorous mind refused to be sidetracked. He kept picturing Kristin, glowing and beautiful in a long white dress and veil, slowly walking up the aisle of St. Paul's to the strains of the wedding march.

Nick had only been inside St. Paul's once, when his fifth-grade class sang carols one Christmas, but he still remembered how lovely the church was and what a perfect backdrop it would be to Kristin's blond beauty.

Waiting at the foot of the altar would be Doug Llewellyn, the man who would forevermore have the right to touch Kristin, to kiss her, to love her...

Nick gritted his teeth.

No.

No.

No!

Then what are you going to do about it?

What *could* he do? It was too late to do anything.

Is it?

Was it?

He'd never even given her the chance to say whether it was too late or not. He'd signed the proxy, thrust it into her hands and then he'd turned tail and run.

Maybe he still *could* ask her...

Are you nuts? This is her wedding day. You had your chance. You blew it. And now it's too damned late to do a thing.

But she wasn't married yet.

It was only nine-thirty in the morning. She wouldn't be married for eight more hours. More than enough time for him to go back to Green River.

Okay, so say you do go back. Say you even manage to see her. What if she laughs at you?

What if she did?

Nick turned off the water. Opened the shower door and reached for his towel. Slowly began to dry himself off.

He would never know until he tried.

"Oh, Kris," Brooke said with an admiring sigh, "you look s...o...o beautiful."

"Do I?" Kristin stared at herself in the full-length mirror. Brooke had just finished buttoning Kristin's wedding dress and had moved back to admire her.

"You know you do. That dress is perfect for you."

Kristin didn't feel beautiful. It had taken every bit of skill and knowledge she possessed to cover up the evidence of the miserable night she'd spent. "I guess I did a good job on makeup."

"Did you have a bad night?"

"Yeah, you could say that."

Brooke bit her bottom lip. "I thought you were going to call Nick."

Kristin smiled wryly. "I did."

"And?"

"And he's gone."

"Gone? You mean, gone back to New York?"

Kristin nodded.

Just then Lindsay opened the door and poked her head inside. "Can I come in?"

Kristin smiled the first real smile of the day. Her daughter looked gorgeous. Her apricot taffeta dress perfectly complemented her golden tones and enhanced the deep brown of her eyes.

Nick's eyes...

Tears threatened.

Oh, Nick, if you could just see her and how beautiful she looks today...

"You look awfully pretty, sweetie," she said softly, trying to keep her voice light.

"So do you," Lindsay said, coming in and closing the door behind her.

Lindsay and Brooke fussed around Kristin for the next few minutes. Kristin let them. And while she let them, she tried to close her mind to everything. Thinking would only lead to more unhappiness.

But Lindsay, so in tune to her at all times, wasn't to be fooled. "Kris, can I ask you something?"

"Of course."

Lindsay looked at Brooke for a moment. "I—I'm not sure if this is a secret."

"It's okay," Kristin said. "Brooke knows all my secrets."

"Remember when you told me about that boy you loved when you were young?" Lindsay said.

Kristin swallowed. "Yes."

"It's Nick, isn't it?"

"Wh-what makes you say that?"

Lindsay rolled her eyes and looked at Brooke again. "I'm not stupid. I figured it out."

After a moment, Kristin said, "Yes, honey, it was Nick."

"Well, if you love Nick, why are you marrying Doug?"

"Good question," Brooke muttered sotto voce.

Kristin gave Brooke a pained look. "Look, Lindsay," she said carefully. "There are things you don't understand. For one thing, I'm not sure Nick still loves me. And for another, it's too late, anyway. He's gone back to New York."

For a moment, neither Lindsay nor Brooke said anything. Then Brooke met Kristin's eyes in the mirror.

"There's no law that says you can't go after him, is there?"

Chapter Fourteen

Kristin picked up the phone.

Ted answered. "Oh, hi, Kristin. Did you want to talk to Doug?"

"Please," she said, wishing her heart would quit racing.

"Hello, darling," Doug said.

"Hello, Doug." She took a deep breath. "Listen, I've got to talk to you."

"Okay. Go ahead."

"No, I mean, in person."

"In person?"

"Yes."

"But Kristin, it's supposed to be bad luck for the groom to see the bride on the day of the wedding."

"I know, but this is really important. Can you come over?"

"Well, sure, but—"

"Please, Doug."

She heard him sigh. "All right. I'll be there in a few minutes." She knew he probably thought she was crazy.

Maybe she was.

Nick drove too fast during the last fifty miles of the trip back to Green River, because he'd hit a horrendous multivehicle accident just outside of Bridgeport on Highway 8, and it had been two hours before the police were able to get it cleared out and traffic routed around it.

So it was almost four o'clock by the time he reached Green River. He headed straight for Kristin's, hoping she'd still be there. He wasn't sure how weddings were handled nowadays, whether brides got ready at home like they used to, or if they dressed at the church.

Well, if she wasn't at the house, he'd go to the church. He almost laughed, imagining the expressions on the faces of her family if he showed up unannounced at the church. Hell, they were probably going to pass out from shock when he showed up at the house. They'd probably try to keep him from seeing Kristin.

Let 'em try, he thought. Now that he'd decided what he was going to do, no one on earth was going to stop him.

Kristin sat on her bed and waited. From time to time, she glanced at Brooke, who sat on the chaise, and Lindsay, who sat on the window seat, and they would give her encouraging smiles.

It had been ten minutes since she'd called Doug. He only lived ten minutes away. At any second, he would be there.

There was a light tapping at the door.

Kristin's gaze flew to Brooke's. Brooke grimaced.

The door opened. "Kristin?"

Meredith walked in, looking the very picture of the elegant mother of the bride in her pale blue raw silk dress and color-coordinated pumps. Her gaze took in all three of them. She frowned. "What are you girls doing? Kristin, I thought you'd be ready by now. Where's your veil?" Not waiting for an answer, she walked over to the large box sitting on the chest at the foot of the bed and opened it. She lifted out the gossamer veil and gave it a little shake. Then, smiling, she walked over to Kristin and placed it carefully on her head.

"There," she said. "It looks wonderful. Don't you think so, Brooke?"

"Yes," Brooke said, "wonderful."

At that exact moment, the doorbell pealed. And kept pealing.

Kristin held her breath.

Lindsay's eyes got big.

Brooke muttered something unintelligible.

"Who on *earth* is making such a racket?" Meredith said. She walked to the open door and out into the hallway. "Milly! Will you *please* answer that door?"

"Yes, ma'am," Milly called.

Kristin looked at Brooke. Brooke made a thumbs-up gesture and smiled at her. Kristin took a deep breath and walked out into the hallway. She could just see the front door from where she stood.

Milly opened it.

Kristin's heart knocked painfully.

Meredith gasped.

It was Nick.

A Nick dressed in jeans and a black turtleneck sweater and looking so handsome, it nearly took her breath away.

He stepped inside. "I'm here to see Kristin," he said in a clear, don't-give-me-any-trouble voice that carried all the way upstairs.

Behind her, Kristin heard Brooke and Lindsay.

"Oh, boy," said Brooke.

"Where is she?" Nick said.

"I'm here, Nick, I'm here," Kristin said, finally finding her voice over her racing heart. She walked to the stairs and started down.

He looked up.

Their eyes met.

And at that precise moment, two things happened. Kristin's father walked out to the entryway from the back of the house, saying, "What's going on out here?" and Doug, dressed in his black tux, stepped in through the open doorway.

For one long, silent moment, no one moved.

And then everyone started talking at once.

"Who let *him* in?" Edmond shouted, rushing toward Nick.

"Kristin, I have to talk to you," Nick said, fending off her father. "Would you come down here, please?"

"Go, Kristin," Brooke urged. "Go."

"Hi, Nick!" Lindsay called.

"Ohmigod," Meredith said. She sat down on the top step and fanned herself.

"Kristin?" Doug said.

"Would anyone like some coffee?" Milly said.

Kristin ignored everyone but Nick. She held her gown up and raced down the stairs. When she reached the bottom, he was there waiting.

A hush fell over the onlookers.

"Kristin," Nick said softly. He touched her cheek. For the first time in the last ten years, he felt uncertain. He loved her so much. "I..." He stopped. Searched her eyes.

And then she smiled. One of her brilliant, beautiful smiles. And he knew it was going to be all right.

"Petrillo," her father said, "I want you to leave. *Right now.*"

Nick turned, faced her father. "Mr. Blair, I love your daughter. I have always loved your daughter, and I think—I *hope*—she still loves me."

Kristin's heart turned over, and tears filled her eyes.

"I know you don't like me," Nick continued, still talking to her father, "and for a long time, I hated you, too. But none of that makes any difference now. So, if it's not too late, and if Kristin will still have me, I intend to do what I should have done years ago. I intend to marry her and love her forever, whether you like it or not.''

Now Kristin's tears *did* fall. "Oh, Nick," she cried. "Of *course* I still love you. I've *always* loved you!"

"Hey, wait a minute," Doug said.

Oh, God, Doug! She'd forgotten about him again. Kristin reached for Nick's hand, then looked at Doug. "Doug, I'm so sorry."

"I can't believe this," Doug said. "Edmond, are you going to allow this?"

"Hell, no, I'm not going to allow it!" her father said, his face reddening.

"Well, Daddy," Kristin said, "I don't see how you're going to stop me. Not this time." She looked at Doug again. "Doug, you don't really love me. I know you don't. We were both entering into this marriage for the wrong reasons, and I think it's time we admitted it.

"If you're honest," Kristin continued relentlessly, "I think you'll admit that you've already gotten what you really wanted. To be president of Blair Manufacturing." With every word, her shoulders felt lighter and lighter. It felt wonderful to finally speak the truth.

Doug clenched his jaw. "If you think so little of me," he said stiffly, "then I think I was just saved from making a huge mistake." Throwing one more glance in her father's direction, he swung around and left.

Kristin realized his words were a way to save his pride. A moment later, she was in Nick's arms.

"Will you marry me?" he said.

"I want to. I want to more than anything in the world, but first we need to talk about something."

His eyes lit up and he grinned. "Talk all you want, but we're getting married." And then, ignoring everyone, he kissed her. Thoroughly. And several times.

"Oh, good," Lindsay piped up. "I like Nick lots better than Doug!"

When Nick let her up for air, Kristin took his hand and faced her parents. "Mom, Dad, I know you're upset, and I'm sorry about that, but I love him."

Her father gave them a long, hard look. For a few moments, Kristin thought he wasn't going to come around. Finally he nodded. His gaze flicked to the stairs, and Kristin wondered if he were looking at her mother...or Lindsay. "Maybe I was wrong," he conceded quietly. "Maybe I shouldn't have interfered." His gaze met Kristin's again. "I—I hope you can forgive me."

Kristin smiled around the lump in her throat. She let go of Nick's hand and walked to her father, throwing her arms around him and hugging him tightly. Whispering into his ear, she said, "I have to tell him about Lindsay."

"I know," her father whispered back.

By now, her mother had walked slowly downstairs. Tears glittered in her eyes. "I'm sorry, too."

"I know you are, Mom."

"We just... We want you to be happy."

Kristin's smile was watery, too. "I am happy. Nick makes me happy."

Then she and her mother hugged.

Finally Kristin turned back to Nick. "Let's go upstairs."

Once they reached the privacy of her room and had shut the door, he reached for her again.

"No, wait," she said. "I have to tell you something first. After I do, you..." She swallowed, suddenly afraid. "You might not want to marry me." She almost laughed. Would have if this were not such a serious moment, because she had said almost the same identical words to Doug a little over a week ago.

"Don't be silly," Nick said tenderly. "Nothing you could say would make me change my mind."

She sat on the side of the bed and patted the space next to her. "This is so hard."

"Kristin..." For the first time, there was a tinge of alarm in his voice. "What?"

She looked up, into those beautiful dark eyes that were so like Lindsay's. The love she felt for him was so strong, it almost hurt to look at him. What would he say when she told him? What would he think? Would he be angry? Would he change his mind? Walk away from her again?

Oh, God, please give me the strength to choose the right words....

"Nick," she said, reaching for his hand. "When you left me all those years ago, I was completely and totally devastated and I—"

"Kristin, love, I know, and I'm sor—"

"Wait," she said. "Please don't interrupt. I—I might lose my courage if you do. Anyway, as you know, I believed you'd taken my father's money and didn't want me. I'm only telling you this again so you'll understand my frame of mind."

He nodded, his eyes never leaving her face.

Kristin drew strength from the warmth of his hand enclosing hers and from the love she saw shining in his eyes. "When we'd been in Europe a couple of weeks, I made a discovery." She squeezed his hand. "I found out I was three months pregnant. I—I had the baby in Switzerland."

For a moment, she wasn't sure he'd heard her, because his expression didn't change. And then, suddenly, his body jerked, and the color drained from his face.

Kristin could hear the little Wedgwood clock her mother had given her ticking merrily from its place on her dresser. She could hear muted voices from downstairs. She could hear a siren somewhere in the distance.

Her heart skipped in fear.

"Lindsay," he said in a strangled voice.

"Yes," Kristin whispered.

He dropped her hand. Stood. Walked to the window and looked out.

Kristin wanted so much to go to him. To put her arms around his rigid body. To hold him and tell him she knew how he must be feeling and how sorry she was.

But she was afraid.

What if he rebuffed her?

What if he couldn't forgive her?

The seconds ticked by.

And Kristin waited. And prayed. She had never been so frightened in her life. If she lost him now...after everything they'd been through...she wasn't sure she could survive.

Just when she thought he might never speak to her again, he turned. His face was still pale, and he wasn't smiling. But he didn't look angry. He looked...stunned. And stunning Kristin, his eyes looked suspiciously bright.

Oh, please, please... Kristin held her breath.

"Lindsay is my daughter?"

"Yes."

Slowly a smile spread across his face. "That terrific kid is *my* daughter?"

Kristin burst into tears. "Y-yes," she blubbered.

Two seconds later, she was in his arms, and they held each other tightly as their tears mingled with their kisses.

A little later, once they'd both become a bit calmer, Kristin said, "Nick, I'm so sorry it all happened this way."

"Don't be sorry. I don't blame you." He shrugged. "Hell, I don't even blame your dad anymore. I'm tired of being angry." He kissed the tip of her nose. "I just want to be happy...to look to the future."

"Oh, that's what I want, too, but I can't help feeling bad about all the years you've missed. Lindsay really is a terrific kid. And she's like you in so many ways."

"Is she?"

The expression on his face was so like Lindsay's when she was happy that Kristin almost started crying again. "Yes," she said softly. "She is."

He closed his eyes and tucked Kristin's head under his chin. He was so filled with happiness, he was afraid the last hour might be a dream and he would wake up and find that none of this had happened after all. "To think," he murmured, "that I almost missed out on all her future years, too." Suddenly he drew back, grinning. "Let's go get her. I can't wait to talk to her. There are so many things we have to get caught up on. She doesn't know about me yet, does she?"

"No, but Nick...wait...we have to talk about this some more." There was an expression in her eyes that frightened him for a second. "I—I want us to tell Lindsay about you and me someday, but I don't think it would be in her best interest for her to know just yet, do you?"

"Why not?"

"Because my parents are the only parents she's

ever known. Finding out about you and me, it's going to be a shock. And she's just a kid. I'm not sure how the news would affect her.''

Nick wanted to protest. He wanted to say it wasn't fair to tell him he had a daughter and then, in the next breath, to say he couldn't acknowledge her. And yet...what Kristin had said made sense. It hurt, but she was right.

He drew her close again and kissed the top of her head. ''You're right. I hate to admit it, but you are.''

''That doesn't mean we can't *ever* tell her,'' Kristin said. ''Just that we need to make sure she's ready to hear it.''

''You don't have any objection to me telling my mother, do you? As long as she doesn't give our secret away?''

''Of course not.''

Nick sighed. ''Now that we've got all that out of the way, will you finally agree to marry me?''

Again she drew back to look at him. ''Before I answer, will you answer a question of mine?''

''Anything.''

''Where are we going to live?''

For a moment, he was taken aback. And then he realized what she was trying to tell him. ''Well, I know one thing,'' he said, stringing out the moment. ''I've missed enough of my daughter's growing-up years. I sure as hell don't intend to miss any more.''

Kristin started to smile.

''We're going to live right here in Green River,''

he said, lifting her up high and swinging her around. "Where we belong. *Now* will you marry me?"

"You just try and stop me," she said just before she lowered her lips to his.

Epilogue

From the pages of the Green River Gazette

"Around the Town"
by Deena Bartholomew

Well, folks, Kristin Blair's wedding is over, and what a wedding it was! The three hundred guests at St. Paul's were stunned to discover there'd been a major change in participants. When the lovely Kristin walked down the aisle on the arm of her father, Edmond Blair, it was to meet another groom entirely from the one she'd been scheduled to marry.

Kristin is now Mrs. Nicholas Edward Petrillo,

who is the son of Peggy Morgan Petrillo and the late James Petrillo of Green River. Nick recently returned to Green River after twelve years in Manhattan, where he's made a name for himself as the manager of the hugely successful Fiske Warburton Fund.

My sources tell me Kristin and Nick were teenage sweethearts whose romance never entirely cooled. Her ex-fiancé, Doug Llewellyn, took the development in stride. When interviewed a few hours after the wedding, he said, "I wish them well." Of course, dear readers, Doug is now president of Blair Manufacturing, not a bad consolation prize at all.

For those of you who wonder how it was possible to switch grooms at the last minute, this reporter was told by the bride's father that a special license was obtained only fifteen minutes before the ceremony started.

The new Mr. and Mrs. Petrillo will honeymoon in Paris and, upon their return, will divide their time between Mr. Petrillo's apartment in Manhattan and the home they plan to build in Green River.

* * * * *

Take 4 bestselling love stories FREE

Plus get a FREE surprise gift!

Special Limited-time Offer

Mail to Silhouette Reader Service™

P.O. Box 609
Fort Erie, Ontario
L2A 5X3

YES! Please send me 4 free Silhouette Special Edition® novels and my free surprise gift. Then send me 6 brand-new novels every month, which I will receive months before they appear in bookstores. Bill me at the low price of $3.71 each plus 25¢ delivery and GST*. That's the complete price and a savings of over 10% off the cover prices—quite a bargain! I understand that accepting the books and gift places me under no obligation ever to buy any books. I can always return a shipment and cancel at any time. Even if I never buy another book from Silhouette, the 4 free books and the surprise gift are mine to keep forever.

335 BPA A3UZ

Name	(PLEASE PRINT)	
Address		Apt. No.
City	Province	Postal Code

This offer is limited to one order per household and not valid to present Silhouette Special Edition® subscribers. *Terms and prices are subject to change without notice.
Canadian residents will be charged applicable provincial taxes and GST.

CSPE-696   ©1990 Harlequin Enterprises Limited

In April 1997
Bestselling Author

DALLAS SCHULZE

takes her Family Circle series to new heights with

TESSA'S CHILD

In April 1997 Dallas Schulze brings readers a
brand-new, longer, out-of-series title featuring the
characters from her popular Family Circle miniseries.

When rancher Keefe Walker found Tessa Wyndham he
knew that she needed a man's protection—she was
pregnant, alone and on the run from a heartless past.
Keefe was also hiding from a dark past...but in one
overwhelming moment he and Tessa forged a family
bond that could never be broken.

Available in April wherever books are sold.

IN CELEBRATION OF MOTHER'S DAY, JOIN
SILHOUETTE THIS MAY AS WE BRING YOU

a funny thing

HAPPENED ON THE WAY TO THE

Delivery Room

THESE THREE STORIES, CELEBRATING THE
LIGHTER SIDE OF MOTHERHOOD, ARE
WRITTEN BY YOUR FAVORITE AUTHORS:

KASEY MICHAELS
KATHLEEN EAGLE
EMILIE RICHARDS

When three couples make the trip to the delivery
room, they get more than their own bundles of
joy...they get the promise of love!

Available this May,
wherever Silhouette books are sold.

Silhouette®
™

MD

As seen on TV!
Free Gift Offer

With a Free Gift proof-of-purchase from any Silhouette® book,
you can receive a beautiful cubic zirconia pendant.

This gorgeous marquise-shaped stone is a genuine cubic
zirconia—accented by an 18" gold tone necklace.

(Approximate retail value $19.95)

Send for yours today...
compliments of  *Silhouette*®

To receive your free gift, a cubic zirconia pendant, send us one original proof-of-purchase, photocopies not accepted, from the back of any Silhouette Romance™, Silhouette Desire®, Silhouette Special Edition®, Silhouette Intimate Moments® or Silhouette Yours Truly™ title available in February, March and April at your favorite retail outlet, together with the Free Gift Certificate, plus a check or money order for $1.65 U.S./$2.15 CAN. (do not send cash) to cover postage and handling, payable to Silhouette Free Gift Offer. We will send you the specified gift. Allow 6 to 8 weeks for delivery. Offer good until April 30, 1997 or while quantities last. Offer valid in the U.S. and Canada only.

Free Gift Certificate

Name: _____

Address: _____

City: _____ State/Province: _____ Zip/Postal Code: _____

Mail this certificate, one proof-of-purchase and a check or money order for postage and handling to: SILHOUETTE FREE GIFT OFFER 1997. In the U.S.: 3010 Walden Avenue, P.O. Box 9077, Buffalo NY 14269-9077. In Canada: P.O. Box 613, Fort Erie, Ontario L2Z 5X3.

FREE GIFT OFFER   **084-KFD**

ONE PROOF-OF-PURCHASE

To collect your fabulous FREE GIFT, a cubic zirconia pendant, you must include this original proof-of-purchase for each gift with the properly completed Free Gift Certificate.

084-KFD

Silhouette
SPECIAL EDITION
™

WELCOME TO
SILVER CREEK COUNTY

A place full of small-town Texas charm, where
everybody knows your name and falling
in love is all in a day's work!

Award-winning author **SHARON DE VITA** has
spun several delightful stories full of matchmaking
kids, lonely lawmen, single parents and humorous
townsfolk! Watch for the first two books,
THE LONE RANGER
(Special Edition #1078, 1/97)
and
THE LADY AND THE SHERIFF
(Special Edition #1103, 5/97).
And there are many more heartwarming
tales to come!

So come on down to Silver Creek and make
a few friends—you'll be glad you did!

ERICA SPINDLER

the bestselling author of
FORTUNE and FORBIDDEN FRUIT

Outrageous and unconventional, Veronique Delacroix is an illegitimate child of one of the oldest and wealthiest families in New Orleans. A gambler by nature, Veronique can never say no to a challenge... especially from Brandon Rhodes, heir to one of the biggest business empires in the country. Thus begins a daring game of romantic roulette, where the stakes may be too high....

"Erica Spindler is a force to be reckoned with in the romance genre." —*Affaire de Coeur*

CHANCES ARE

Available in May 1997 at your favorite retail outlet.